# Hangin' Out with Cici

## *or*

# My Mother Was Never a Kid

*Francine Pascal*

LAUREL-LEAF BOOKS

LAUREL-LEAF BOOKS bring together under a single imprint outstanding works of fiction and nonfiction particularly suitable for young adult readers, both in and out of the classroom. Charles F. Reasoner, Professor Emeritus of Children's Literature and Reading, New York University, is consultant to this series.

Published by
Dell Publishing Co., Inc.
1 Dag Hammarskjold Plaza
New York, New York 10017

To Johnny

Laurel-Leaf Library  ¦ TM 766734, Dell Publishing Co., Inc.

ISBN: 0-440-93364-1

RL: 5.6

Reprinted by arrangement with Viking Penguin, Inc.

Printed in the United States of America

First Laurel-Leaf printing—March 1985

# One

Getting to be thirteen turned out to be an absolute and complete bummer. I mean it. What a letdown. You wouldn't believe the years I wasted dreaming about how sensational everything was going to be once I was a teen-ager. The way I pictured it, the change was going to be fantastic. Overnight, people would stop treating me like some dumb little kid. Instead I'd be respected pretty much as a pre-adult, practically running my own life. Sure, I'd still have to live at home, but mostly I'd be making my own decisions. Oh, occasionally my parents would ask me to do something, but it wouldn't be an order—it'd be more like a suggestion.

Hah!

"Victoria, that room is a pigsty. I want it cleaned up immediately or you can forget about sleepovers for a month." That's my mother suggesting. "And another thing," she says, adding three more little nuggets of friendly advice, "see that your laundry is put away before you empty the dishwasher and don't leave the house without walking Norman." That's our sheepdog. "And Victoria? . . ."

"Yes, Mother."

". . . Put on your jacket. It's only May."

Wow! I must have been some jerk. Truth is nothing's changed except that maybe now I won't have to listen to that bull about waiting till I'm a teen-ager. Fact is, now they use it against me. "That certainly wasn't proper behavior for a teen-ager." And I'm still waiting. "A bike tour is a wonderful idea, but you'll have to wait until you're at least sixteen." Of course when I'm sixteeen they'll have moved all the good things to eighteen, and then when I get there, it'll be twenty-one. I'll always be waiting to be old enough for this or that until I'm ninety. *Then* they'll say, "That's something you should have done when you were seventeen or twenty." It seems like you're always the wrong age. What a relief to know that in just three weeks I'll have a birthday. Fourteen has got to be better.

Except, of course, if you have a mother like mine. You wouldn't believe how overprotective she is. Do you know that I'm the only kid in the whole eighth grade who can't go to the movies at night? And then she takes every little thing so seriously. Like what happened yesterday in school. I can understand her being a little upset, but in my opinion she overreacted. After all, it was the first time in my whole life that I ever got suspended. For practically nothing. And besides, I wasn't the only one involved. There were eight of us and just because I was the only one suspended doesn't mean it was all my fault. Which, in fact, it wasn't.

Personally I think it was mostly Mrs. Serrada's fault. (In case you didn't know, she's the grossest English teacher in the Western Hemisphere.) But what can you expect at Brendon School? That's this really uptight private school I go to. The kind of yes-sir, no-sir place where they make you wear these horrendous uniforms every day. You should see them—gray skirts with fat ugly box pleats and a vomity blue blazer with a scratchy gold emblem on the pocket that everybody always says looks like an eagle sitting on a toilet. It's all a terrible embarrassment, and of course, I detest it like crazy. A lot of good that does. I've been going there since third grade. Anyway, back to what happened yesterday. There probably wouldn't have been any trouble if dear old Serrada hadn't picked such a boring movie for our one and only class trip all term. Actually I've got nothing against Shakespeare; in fact I think he's pretty okay sometimes. He did a super job with Romeo and Juliet (the movie anyway) but Richard the Second? Gross.

Anyway, all we did was sneak up to the balcony, goof around a little, throw a couple of gum wrappers over the railing, and smoke one cigarette. That was the worst. The cigarette, I mean. I really inhaled it deep and it made me so nauseous and dizzy that I thought I was going to fall right into the orchestra. The thought scared me so much that I slid down to the floor and just sat there waiting for my head to clear. Unfortunately, my friend Liza didn't see me, and when she tripped over my leg she grabbed Danielle and she fell too, and then everyone started fooling around and falling down. Well, everybody started laughing like crazy. And I guess we got a little noisy because Mrs. Serrada turned around to see what was going on and spotted me holding the cigarette. And that's when Tina Osborne shot the rolled gum wrapper. Tina swears she wasn't aiming at Mrs. Serrada, but it hit her smack on the forehead just the same. Far out! You should have seen old Fatso come charging up the stairs to the balcony. We all jumped up and started to scramble down the opposite staircase, but we were laughing so hard we kept stumbling into each other.

I guess the manager must have heard all the commotion because the next thing you know, the house lights go on and we're caught. What a hassle Fatso made about the whole thing, especially the cigarette. Nickie Rostivo tried to lighten it a little by telling her that one cigarette for

eight people wasn't too dangerous. I even pointed out that
we were in the smoking section. That did it. That's when
she exploded. Normally she's got a very soft voice, kind
of sick-sweet, but when she loses her temper she sounds
like a lumberjack. It's really weird to hear that big voice
boom out of such a small fat muffin of a woman. "How
dare you disgrace the school blah blah blah . . . How
could you be so rude . . . untrustworthy" et cetera, et
cetera and on and on. By now the rest of the class was
jammed halfway up the steps dying to find out what was
going on. Even the nosy movie manager squeezed his way
through to get a better look. That's when I started to break
up—I mean, seeing his bald head sticking out from the
middle of all those kids really flipped me out. I tried to
cover the giggles by pretending to have a coughing fit,
which probably made it sound even worse. Of course
everyone turned to stare at me and of course that really
finished me off. "And what, may I ask, is so amusing?"
says Mrs. Serrada in snake spit. "Tell us, Victoria, so that
we all may enjoy the joke."

Naturally, there's nothing funny, but I can't tell her that
because I'm laughing too hard. It's so embarrassing. But I
can't help it. These laughing fits happen to me at the worst
possible times and once I start I can't stop. Sometimes it
happens to me at the dinner table and it's really awful.
Some stupid thing (it can even be really serious or sad)
will strike me funny and I start to laugh. It doesn't last too
long if nobody pays any attention, but if someone, like my
dad, tells me to stop, I'm dead. I become hysterical and of
course he becomes furious because he thinks I'm laughing
at him and he'll invariably send me to my room until I can
control myself. You'd think by now they'd understand that
it doesn't mean anything and just leave me alone to get
over it by myself.

Like with the trouble at school. Sure, I know it was a dumb thing to do, but mostly it was just silly and nobody got hurt and Fatso shouldn't have suspended me. Big deal, so I got hysterical. I would have apologized later. I mean, it wasn't so terrible that she had to suspend me. And naturally that brought the smoke rising from my mother's hair when they told her about it later.

Anyway, I wasn't too scared in the theater. In fact, it was all pretty exciting—you know, all of us in it together. Some of the other kids who weren't involved felt sort of left out, and everybody was coming up to us and wanting to know what happened and all that. By the time we got back to class, the story was all over the school and what a story it turned into! One version had Nickie Rostivo dangling from the balcony by one hand and all the rest of us smoking, and not plain old cigarettes either, and making out like crazy. Since I was the only one who got suspended, naturally I was the star. Actually it was kind of fun being a celebrity.

Until I got home. You know, it's a funny thing but I actually thought my mother might, just once, be on my side a little. After all, I'm the one who really got it the worst and I didn't do anything that much different from the others. I don't think it was fair to take it all out on me and I told her so, and I really and truly expected her to agree. Hah! What a pipe dream. She was furious with me. What does she care what's fair or unfair? All she wanted to know was whether I thought sneaking up to that balcony was right or wrong. I said of course I knew it was wrong. "Then," she said, "why did you do it?" How come she can't understand that it's not that simple? Doesn't she remember what it's like when all your friends are involved in something goofy, not really terrible, just a little nutty and a lot of fun? What does she want me to do—say no like some goody-goody? I was dumb to expect any sympathy from her. Still, the worst I thought would happen was that I'd be grounded for a couple of days like everyone else. But not my mother. She has to treat me like some kind of dumb five-year-old. First she tells me that I can't watch TV or have any sleepovers for the next month. I don't like that, but it's not the end of the world. Then she says, get this, I'm not allowed to talk on the phone for a whole week. Furthermore, when anyone calls she's going to tell them that I can't come to the phone because I'm being punished. Is that the most embarrassing thing you've ever heard? I'm never going to be able to face anyone ever again. But she doesn't care. She'd probably like it if I stayed right here in my bedroom, sitting on my stupid canopied bed until it was time for college.

Wouldn't you know it, the phone's ringing right now. I'll bet it's for me. Naturally my mother has to answer on the hall extension right outside my room. She wants to make sure I hear her. Oh, God! It's Michael Langer, a really cute guy from high school, and she's telling him how I can't come to the phone because I'm being punished. How could she? I'm steaming mad, and as soon as I hear her hang up, I stamp my foot real hard and scream, "I hate you!"

The first time I told her that I was very little and she got terrifically upset. Her eyes were all watery and she took me on her lap and we talked for a long time until I finally told her that I really loved her. Since then she's read that all children feel like that sometimes and it's healthy to let them say it.

Now she comes stumping toward my room, saying, "You just listen to me!" She's angry and just pushes the door open without even knocking. "You're behaving like a four-year-old."

And we start our usual argument. "That's the way you treat me," I say, and she tells me that's because I act like one and I should realize I was wrong and accept my punishment, and it goes on that way with me saying one thing and her saying another but never really answering me. Like I say that I don't mind being punished, but it's embarrassing to have all my friends know about it, and she says, "Well, you should have thought of that first." That's what I mean. What kind of an answer is that? Oh, what's the use, she doesn't even try to understand me and there's nothing I can do about it.

I swear I'll never treat my daughter the way they treat me. I'll really be able to understand her because I'll remember how awful it was for me. I'll never do anything to embarrass her and I'll never make her cry. I'll be her best friend and never lose my temper with her even if she makes mistakes like forgetting a dentist appointment or being late for dinner or getting a bad mark on a science test. I'll just talk to her and try to understand why these things happened, and even if I can't, I'll never get angry with her no matter what, and never yell at her and never punish her, never, not ever.

I can't believe my mother was ever my age. I think she was born a mother. Or if she was ever a kid, she must have been perfect. Unless maybe things were so completely different in the olden days that kids didn't do any thinking on their own, they just did exactly what they were told. I picture my mother exactly like a girl in my class, Margie Sloan, a revolting goody-goody who wouldn't dream of ever sneaking up to a balcony or even handing in a paper a minute late. Everyone agrees that Margie is the most boring person in the entire school and she's never invited to parties or even just for sleepovers. That's probably the way my mother was. No wonder we can't get along. We're just not the same type.

There's another thing that really bugs me about my mother. The way she talks. "If I have to raise my voice one more time I'm going to blah blah blah." Or, "How dare you . . . who do you think you are?" and "If I ever catch you doing that again blah blah blah," and so on. She has about ten of these beauties and they never change. She always sounds like a mother, an angry mother. God, I hope I don't grow up like her. And I really despise it when everybody compares me to her. "Oh, you're the perfect image of your mother." Naturally it's always one of my mother's friends who says it. If one of my friends said it I'd kick her in the shin.

The worst part about it is that it's sort of true. We do have the same kind of pushed-up nose and the same color eyes and supposedly we have the same smile though I really don't see that at all. Actually, I guess it wouldn't be the worst thing in the world if I looked like her when I grow up because she's pretty all-right-looking. But that's it. I mean, I absolutely don't want to be like her in any way.

Boy, did I get stuck when you consider some of the great mothers around. Like my friend Steffie's mother. Now, she's absolutely super. I feel like I can say anything to her at all because she's such an understanding person. And she's fun, too. When Steffie and I ice-skate at the Wollman Rink, I actually don't mind if her mother comes along. I wouldn't hate being her daughter at all. In fact, I'd love it. Beats me why Steffie says she can't stand her.

The phone's ringing again. More embarrassment. Then I hear my mother say, "Oh, hello, Mr. Davis." It's going to be worse than embarrassing because there's only one Mr. Davis I know and that's the new principal at school.

He's only been here six months but already nobody can stand him. I think the phone call's going to be disaster.

"Uh-huh . . . uh-huh . . . uh-huh." That's my mother. He's probably saying a whole lot of vicious, awful things about me and she's agreeing. Even if they're not out-and-out lies, they're certainly horrendous exaggerations because he absolutely hates me. I mean a hundred people can be doing something wrong and he'll only pick me out. He really has it in for me. I'm not saying he's 100 percent wrong or that I should get medals for them, but they're not that big a deal. Like that time when I got caught playing hooky, Marie and Betsy both said they were going to come with me. And the business with the paint on the blackboard. There were four of us in on that in the beginning and it was only because Tommy Agrasso was absent that day that I had to be the one to steal the paint from the art class. I admit I thought up the idea of smearing glue on the keys of the auditorium piano, but that evened out because I was the one they made scrub it off. And as for always talking in the classrooms, everybody in the whole world does that and it's too trivial to even mention.

My mother's talking very low on the phone to Mr. Davis, but finally she hangs up and I can tell by the bang that I'm in big trouble. She charges into my room. Not only doesn't she knock, she practically takes the whole door down with her, she's in such a fury.

"Do you know who that was?"

"Yeah."

"Yes," she hisses. In the middle of everything she has to correct my grammar.

"Yes," I repeat because things are bad enough already.

"That was the principal."

"How is he?"

"Don't be smart!"

You see how hopeless it is? I was only being polite.

"You aren't being suspended. . . ."

"Oh, wow! Did I misjudge that nice old guy. . . ."

"It's worse than that. They don't want you back at all. You make too much trouble for them. They feel you're—how did he put it?—in the wrong learning environment."

Groan. Sickening thud as my stomach drops to my knees. Kicked out!

"They can't do that," I blurt.

"Why not?" My mother's eyes are practically smoldering. "Tell me why not."

I'm afraid to look at her.

"You apparently think you can do anything in the world that *you* want. Why can't the school? Why shouldn't you get thrown out? You cause nothing but unhappiness and embarrassment and . . . ."

Suddenly she kind of sinks down on the edge of the bed and buries her face in her hands for a couple of seconds. I hear a deep, long sigh. Finally she raises her head and stares right into my eyes. I never have the guts to look back, especially if I'm feeling guilty. Instead I get real busy brushing invisible things off my jeans or concentrating on nothing in the middle of my empty palm.

"Victoria," she says after a couple of seconds, "are you deliberately trying to hurt us, your father and me?"

"No." Very small voice.

"Then why do you keep doing all these awful things? Please, tell me."

I wish I could tell her, but all I can do is shrug my shoulders and say, "I don't know." Because honestly, I don't. I mean, these things never seem so terrible when I'm doing them, it's only later, when they get so blown up that I know I shouldn't have done them, but then, of course, it's too late. But that's me. Always goofing up.

You should hear me with the boys. I say the dumbest things. Even the way I look is all wrong. I must have spent ninety million allowances on face gook and my complexion is still horrendous, my hair looks dirty two seconds after I wash it, and my knees are so bony that I'll probably have to wear jeans the rest of my life. Oh, what's the use? I could go on forever. The thing is, I'm a mess. Also, it's horrific the way I don't know where I'm supposed to be. I mean, I'm certainly not a little kid like my sister Nina, but nobody lets me be as grown-up as I feel inside. Of course, there's no point trying to tell my mother these things. She'd just say I looked fine and probably blame it on adolescence, like it was some kind of disease. Maybe it is.

"I hate to keep punishing you," my mother says, shaking her head and looking just a little bit sad. "I wish there were some other way."

"Well, I don't know . . ." I mumble. Why do I always grope like a jerk when I want to say something important? "I guess you could try to understand me a little better." I expect to hear her say, "I understand you perfectly" or something like that. But she surprises me.

"All right, Victoria, I'll try. What is it I don't understand?"

Oh, God, what a question. Doesn't she know there's no way to answer?

"Well?"

"Me."

"Okay. What is it I don't understand about you? This is serious, Victoria, so let's talk about it. Tell me what I'm doing wrong."

Now she wants to talk—when she's got me on the torture rack. That's just like her. How come she always gets to pick the time for these little chats?

"You have to tell me what's on your mind, Victoria. I can't do it without your help."

See? It's hopeless. I mean how am I going to help her when I don't know what's going on either? I finally say, "Well, you don't ever let me live my own life. I'm not a baby, I can take care of myself. But all you do is keep treating me like a child. I'm not a child. I'm an . . . I feel I'm as adult as a real adult."

I really don't want to go on, but she doesn't interrupt and kind of forces me to keep talking. Maybe I'd do it anyway. Sometimes I'm a real motormouth.

"Like, I hear what you and Mrs. Weinstein and the Elliotts and all your other friends talk about when they come over," I blabber on. "The movies, television, why you don't like Mr. Bailey, where the good places are to eat, and things like that. What's so adult about that? Those are the same things I talk about with my friends. I mean, I don't see any difference." I take a deep breath so I can keep rattling on, but the fact is I can't think of anything else to say.

"All right," my mother says. "You have a point. A lot of things you and I do are pretty much alike. I'll even call them adult things. But how about this? Suppose I came home and you asked me what I did this afternoon and I said, oh, I was with the Weinsteins and the Elliotts and all my friends at the movies and we spent the whole time secretly smoking and giggling and running up the aisles and throwing spitballs. What would you think, Victoria? That I was behaving like an adult? Do adults do that? Do they?"

Naturally I'm not going to answer that one.

"So you're not an adult yet, Victoria. And if you think you are, then the misunderstanding's on your part. I'm not saying you're a child either. You're something in between.

It's a difficult time and I'm sorry, but until you're a lot more mature than you are, you need supervision. And that includes punishment when you do very childish and very bad things.''

"I don't do very bad things." I pout. "Or anyway I don't do them on purpose. That's another thing you don't understand. They're just normal nothings that go a little wrong.''

"You mean to say that all those things that happen are . . . are what? Accidents?''

"Not exactly. I just mean that I don't cause all that trouble on purpose. Besides, mostly they're just little things and I don't know why everybody always gets so excited about them. Like today . . .''

"A perfect example. Because of your shenanigans today the entire movie was ruined for everyone. Are you going to tell me *that* was an accident?''

"But it was, sort of. I mean, nobody meant to ruin the movie. All we wanted to do was sit in the balcony. You know, Mommy, it's really gross the way they treat us like such babies when we go on a class trip. It's positively horrendous when you're almost fourteen to have to march through the streets in a double line. And then in the movie they never let us sit next to our friends and you can't talk and you can't buy candy. And if you do some little thing like changing your seat without asking, they practically freak out.''

"According to Mr. Davis, you weren't just out of your seat, you were smoking and creating a ruckus.''

"So all Mrs. Serrada had to do was shush us and we would have been quiet. Instead she comes charging up the steps like some bull elephant . . .''

"*Victoria!*" She doesn't even let me finish. "You were breaking the rules. Can't you understand that?''

Rules. How come adults are always so hung up on rules? Even if I tell my mother that a lot of Mrs. Serrada's rules are really dumb, she'll still say, "That's no excuse for breaking them." Except I think it is. Boy, if they let kids make the rules things would be a lot better. I'd probably never get into trouble.

"Well? Can't you?"

"Huh?"

"Can't you understand that you were breaking the rules?"

"I didn't exactly think of it that way. Anyway, it wasn't all my fault."

"Of course not. It's never your fault, is it? It's always somebody else's. The teacher's. Or the principal's. All the complaints they've had about you in school, none of them are your fault, are they? Everybody's picking on you."

See, I told you, no matter how many kids are involved, I'm the one who always gets blamed the most, and it's not fair, and now they want to throw me out into the street, and my whole life is ruined, and maybe I should just run away and make them all feel sorry for what they did.

My mother says: "Mr. Davis is setting up an appointment for us at school. We will go visit him and you will be very humble and very sweet. I'll try to straighten this whole matter out. I don't know how successful I'll be. Mr. Davis sounded pretty final about not wanting you back. You're too disruptive. But we'll try because the only other alternative would be a boarding school."

"I won't go!" I blurt it out. I know all about boarding schools. My friend Monica's sister Laura had to go away to one called the Barley School someplace up in Maine, and I heard they beat you and make you go to bed at eight o'clock and scrub the floors every morning. I'd rather die. As it is I'm crying like crazy already.

"Come on now, Victoria," my mother says, pushing a couple of wet strands of hair back of my face. "Boarding schools aren't anything like those awful places you see in the movies."

"I'll run away. I will!" Which is what I thought about doing anyway except this time it's real.

"Calm down for a minute and listen to me. Actually Daddy and I have talked about it before all this, and it might be the best thing that could happen to you. These places are fabulous, like sleep-away camps, only they have classes. You'd probably end up loving it. There's a wonderful school called the Barley School up in New England. Laura Baer went there and she loved it." Of course I know better, but I'm too destroyed to argue.

"I'll hate it," I sob.

"There's no point in discussing it until after we've seen the principal. In the meantime I want you right here in the house where I can keep an eye on you all weekend. I'm sorry to have to punish you, but you have certainly earned it."

And, just like that, she walks out of the room. Can you believe that? My whole life is coming to an end and she won't even let me talk about it. That absolutely proves she doesn't care one iota about me. None of them do. I suppose my sister Nina does a little. But who wants an eleven-year-old pain in the ass on your side?

Oh my God! "Hey, Mom, Ma!" I cry dashing into the hall.

"What now?"

"The party down at Liz's!"

"I told you. I want you home all weekend. You can forget about going to Philadelphia."

"But Ma! She's expecting me. My own cousin. The party's practically in my honor."

"Out of the question. Now go wash your face and comb your hair—Grandma's coming."

I know it's going to be futile but I've got to try to convince her. I've been counting on going to that party for two months and my heart would crack right in two if I couldn't make it. Still, for once in my life, I play it cool. I don't say another word. I just head straight for the bathroom like she said and do my best to wash the crying look off my face and even pull my hair tight back with an elastic band just the way she likes it. By the time I'm finished I hear my grandmother in the living room. What a drag!

Don't get me wrong. I'm crazy about my grandmother. She's absolutely the greatest. But you know how grandparents are, they take everything so seriously. All she has to know is that I've been suspended from school and she'll probably be up all night worrying.

Wait a minute! I don't have to tell her. My mother certainly isn't about to bring it up, so how's she going to know?

"Victoria, darling," says my grandmother as soon as she sees me, "what's the matter? Your eyes are all red. Are you sick?" And she's up in a flash testing my forehead for fever. "I told you she looked a little green the other day, Felicia," she says to my mother, and there's just a hint of accusation in her voice like maybe they're not feeding me enough or something.

"No, Grandma, I'm fine."

"You don't look so fine to me. You look like you've been crying. What's wrong? Did you have trouble in school today?"

I must be the easiest person in the whole world to nail. Nothing left to do but tell the whole gruesome story again. Ugh. I can see that my mother is embarrassed but I wade right in, and just when I'm at the part where it's so unfair that I was the only one suspended, the phone rings. Naturally I jump up to answer it.

"Oh, no you don't, young lady," says good old Mom. "When I say no phone calls, I mean no phone calls." And with the steam rising from the top of her head, my mother storms out of the room to answer the phone. I pray it's not for me.

"Boy, is she mean!" I say to my grandmother.

"Being suspended is a very serious matter, dear, I can see she's very upset." That's one of the beautiful things about my grandmother. She always sounds like she loves me. Like calling me dear and talking so sweetly even if she doesn't agree with me. And we don't agree all the time mostly because she's, you know, sort of proper and old-fashioned sometimes. But she never really loses her patience or gets angry at me.

"Every time I get caught in something the school makes such a big deal about it. They're always suspending me for nothing at all."

"You mean this isn't the first time?"

"Well, not exactly. But you can't really count that other time because it wasn't my fault. I just happened to be there when the trouble started."

"Maybe it wasn't, but you must admit, dear, you do seem to be in the wrong place at the wrong time more often than just about anyone else."

"I guess I'm just unlucky. How come my mother can't look at things the way you do instead of always flying off the handle?"

"I used to do some pretty fancy flying off the handle when your mother and Uncle Steve were children. They could be very irritating at times."

I can believe that about my mother. She irritates me all the time. But Uncle Steve? Grandma has to be kidding.

He's the best uncle in the whole world. I can practically talk to him like a friend. He's in the advertising business and knows everybody and he's always getting tickets for us to shows and concerts and everything. Mom has him over to dinner a couple of times a month (he's divorced) and always cooks something special for him. I know she's his sister but I always think of him more as my friend than her brother, if that makes any sense. That's probably because he treats me practically like an adult. You know how most adults don't really listen to kids or take them seriously? Well, he's just the opposite. Boy, is my mother lucky to have him for a brother.

"Yes indeed," my grandmother is saying. "Being a mother can be a very hard job."

"Well, it doesn't look so tough to me."

"But it is. Imagine being solely responsible for another person."

"She doesn't *have* to be so responsible for me. I can take care of myself a lot better than she thinks."

"You seem to have slipped up a little today."

"Yeah, well . . ."

"And the other times?"

"Maybe it's like you said. I was in the wrong place at the wrong time."

"Maybe. And possibly when you get older that will happen less and less. But in the meantime somebody's got to take very good care of someone who's so unlucky, and that, my dear, is a full-time job, with a lot of close watching and plenty of worrying. Believe me, Victoria, that can make even the best mother a little mean sometimes."

"Still, I bet you wouldn't be if you were my mother."

My grandmother smiles and starts to say something, but then my mother comes back so she changes her mind.

"That was Mr. Davis calling," my mother says to me.

"Our appointment is for nine o'clock Monday morning. I suggest you think very hard over the weekend about what you're going to say to him."

"Speaking of the weekend," Grandma says, "what train are you making to Elizabeth's tomorrow, Victoria?" I guess my mother didn't tell her about me not going.

"Mommy says I can't go because of the school thing." I've got the feeling this may be my last chance so I play it big. You know those hound dogs that always look like they're going to cry? That's a giggle compared to my face right now.

"Well, that's a shame," my grandmother says to my mother.

"It certainly is and I hope she learns something this time."

"Elizabeth will be so disappointed." Now I'm not saying my grandmother winked or smiled or did anything big like that, but I just got this vibe from her that is definitely good stuff.

"I know," says my mother, "and I feel terrible to have to disappoint her . . ."

". . . Especially on her birthday." God bless Grandma.

"I don't know what to do about that."

"Oh, why don't you let her go . . . for Elizabeth's sake?"

I gotta not smile. I gotta not smile. I gotta not smile.

"You're probably right. I certainly don't want this to be a punishment for Elizabeth." She looks at me and says, "Why should she suffer just because you don't know the difference between right and wrong?"

I almost leap at my mother and kiss her for letting me go. Instead I give my grandmother a huge kiss and shoot out of the room to start packing.

## *Two*

I'm taking a morning train tomorrow. I can hardly wait.
I'm going to get away from this whole grungy scene and
visit my favorite cousin, Liz, down in Philadelphia. She's
almost a year older than me, but we get along great. I was
down there for Christmas vacation and we had a fantastic
time. There was this boy David (he's sixteen), a friend of
Liz's boyfriend, who really liked me. Of course he thought
I was a lot older than thirteen. Everyone thinks I'm very
mature for my age so it was easy to fool him. Anyway, we
went to a party at his friend's house, and when they turned
out the light, he kissed me. Some jerk turned it on again a
couple of minutes later and we were still kissing. It was
such a long kiss that I thought I was going to faint from
holding my breath so long. But it helps. Holding your
breath, I mean. Then you don't think so much about how
your lips are squashing into your braces.

I'll never forget one of the girls at the party. Her name
is Cindy and she's fifteen and thinks she's really hot stuff.
A lot of the boys do too, mostly because she's very
overdeveloped. I mean her breasts are gigantic. Liz says
that she has a terrible reputation and that the boys only like
her because she lets them go pretty far. I don't think I
could ever let a boy touch my breasts unless we were
really in love and then it would have to be on the outside

of my clothes. Sometimes I put my own hand on myself, you know, just to see how it feels. It's not bad. but nothing special. But that's probably because it's me touching me. A couple of times Steffie and I were fooling around pretending to be movie stars and we'd make fun of a love scene. We always start off goofing around and laughing a lot but then it would get kind of serious in the clinches. Don't laugh, but I sort of liked it when she put her hands on my breasts. It felt sort of, I don't know, tingly. That's when we'd stop. I was always a little embarrassed afterward even though she is my best friend and it was only a fooling-around game. I think she felt the same way because we never talked about it and we usually share everything.

David, the boy from Philly, wrote to me when I got back to New York. It was an okay letter, nothing really personal, but he did ask when I was coming down for another visit. I wrote him that I would be down for the weekend of May seventeenth for Liz's birthday and that he was invited to the party. He never answered but Liz said she saw him and he told her that he'd be there. I hope so because right now I don't like any of the boys in my class except maybe Nickie Rostivo and he doesn't even come up to my shoulder. He's cute, but I feel like his mother.

And speaking of mothers, here comes mine click click click down the hall and (without knocking) into my room to say that she and Daddy are going to drive Grandma home and then go to a movie. That means that no one will be home except Nina and me, so I ask her about answering the phone. "Nina is quite capable of answering the phone," she says, talking in that fancy cold voice she uses when she's angry at me. To me, the only thing Nina is quite capable of is being a huge pain in the ass. But at least she knows I'm the boss and of course the first thing I do is make her take the phone off the hook. Most of the time Nina does anything I want. I mean anything. Like one time a whole load of kids from school came back to my house and we were sitting around talking and listening to music when one of the boys got the bright idea that we ought to stage a striptease. Of course, none of us were about to take off our clothes so I got Nina and I told her, "Lucky you, you're the star." And you know what? That jerk actually did it. It was really hysterical with her streaking through the house stark naked. Too much. Finally she hid in the hall closet and wouldn't come out until everyone went home. If I told her to jump off the roof she probably would. She's so dumb.

Actually, that naked thing was probably a little much. I've always felt kind of bad pushing her into it like that because I think I really embarrassed her. To tell you the truth, I only hate Nina some of the time. Mostly because she can never keep a secret and she drives me batty the way she's always hanging around me and my friends. If I leave my door open even a crack she just sort of seeps in. She's so quiet that sometimes I don't even know she's there, but then I'll feel someone staring at me and ugh . . . she's so weird. She even looks weird. She's got the skinniest, boniest legs, glasses that keep slipping down her ski-jump nose, and stringy red hair. She'll probably be okay when she grows up, but right now she's an embarrassment. For that matter, so are my parents. I just hate to have them come up to school or accompany our class on trips. I'm always worried that they're going to do something horrible in front of everybody like taking my hand when we cross the street or making me drink milk instead of Coke at lunchtime. It never actually happens, but that's the way I feel so I hardly ever tell them about parent things at school.

My mother is a sculptor and we have her stuff all over the house. I don't mind that so much because she's really pretty good at it. Last year she had two pieces in the Museum of Modern Art. Those are about the only two pieces I don't like because they're not really much of anything, just forms. Mostly she does heads and they usually look pretty lifelike. She's done four heads of me. The ones she did when I was little were super, but the one she did last year looked more like her than me. I hated it. Another thing about my mother. She's an absolute tennis freak and as far back as I can remember she's been bugging me to take lessons. So finally last summer I said okay and now it beats me why she was so hot for me to learn because she hardly ever plays with me. Naturally when she does, she always creams me without even half trying. Still, I wouldn't mind playing with her a little more. Just for the practice, of course.

My dad's a lawyer. Not the exciting kind who works in court with murderers and juries. The dull kind. He's into real-estate law of some kind. Sometimes at dinner he'll tell my mother a whole long story about one of his cases and you should see how she hangs on every word. She never listens to me like that. Personally, I think she's full of baloney, about being so interested, I mean. Really, who could be so fascinated by things like tax shelters and depreciation? It's ridiculous things like that that give me my laughing fits.

You probably think I spend a lot of time talking and thinking about my mother and you're right. But I can't help it. She seems to be all over my life. Not so much my father. He's pretty okay. Actually he can even be fun sometimes. Like with Coney Island. Every spring he takes us there for the whole day and he lets us go on any ride we want. You know how most fathers are. They just kind of stand off and watch, but not him. He goes on all the rides with us and even into those crazy horror houses. You have to see him, he's really hysterical. We have the best time and he never makes us leave until we're absolutely ready. He can really be pretty nice when he wants to be. But not my mother. She just ruins everything for me, always telling me what I should do and what I forgot to do, and even if by chance I did remember, how it was all wrong anyway. Thank God Grandma came today. I'll have a whole stupendous totally free weekend where I won't have to listen to all that junk.

I don't know about you, but whenever I have something special to look forward to I can't stop thinking about it. Like this weekend and the party. I've been working it over in my head all week, especially at night. I lie awake for hours thinking about what I'll wear, what I'll say and do, and almost every little tiny thing that could possibly happen. Even some impossible things. I create little scenes and play them over and over again like a movie in my head. Naturally, I'm the star and everyone is madly in love with me and I look absolutely perfect and my dancing is spectacular (you know, the kind where everyone forms a ring around you) and my conversation is too much. With dreams like that, the real party is bound to be a bomb. Most of them are anyway. I mean, like the boys stand at one end of the room goofing around, punching each other on the shoulders and laughing like real jerks, and the girls sit on the other side whispering dumb things about the boys. The music blasts away, but nobody dances, and it's too loud for conversation. The only time anyone ever gets together is for a kissing game and that stinks too because most of the time you have to kiss gross guys you really can't stand. And even if you do get to kiss someone you really like, it's never as good as you think it's going to be. I don't know why I always look forward to these parties so much. But I do.

Like with Liz's party this weekend. I'm so anxious to split for Philly I'm up at 6 a.m. It freaks me out when that happens, but it does all the time. All I have to be is a little excited over something and either I can't sleep or I wake up at some ridiculous hour in the morning, and then forget it, I absolutely can't go back to sleep. Today it's not too bad because I only have three hours to kill before the train and there's a new hair style I want to try where you part it really high on the left and let this big loopy wave sort of dangle over your right eyebrow. I saw it in an old movie poster in Brentano's—some lady named Veronica Lake, I think—and Steffie says I have just the right hair for it and that it's very sexy and I'd look twenty years old or at least fifteen. So I can work on that in front of the mirror and then have some breakfast, and three hours aren't that hard to kill anyway.

The haircomb is too much. I love it. Liz is going to freak out when she sees it. It's almost seven-thirty and my mother comes into the kitchen, takes one look at my hair, makes a "you-must-be-out-of-your-mind" face, and says, "I hope you're not going to wear that outside."

She says a couple of more gems and I end up putting my hair back in a straight old part.

I really feel like I want to argue about it with my mother but I don't for two very good reasons. One, I'll lose. Two, I can always dump the old way and go back to the Veronica look on the train. But I can't stay quiet about her next "suggestion." She insists that my bratty little sister come with us to the station to see me off on the train. What for? Who needs her? Is the train going to stay in the station until the engineer gets the go-ahead from Nina?

I say to my mother very reasonably:

"I'll vomit if she comes along."

My mother responds:

"Tell your Aunt Hilda I'll call her on Sunday."

I say:

"Why does that ugly little creep have to come with us anyway?"

She says:

"We won't discuss it. You should be pleased your own sister thinks enough of you to want to see you off. It's a compliment."

I say:

"She's just doing it to spite me. She knows I hate every gut in her body and I don't think it's fair for you to drag her along just because she wants to come. What about me? I don't want her to come. How come you always side with her?" Et cetera, et cetera. When it comes to Nina I could go on forever.

"Finish your breakfast," says my mother, who never cares what I think.

That's when I almost go into a tantrum. Luckily I catch it just in time. The next words out of my mouth are going to be, "If she comes to the station, I'm not going!" And then my mother would say, "It's just as well, Philadelphia is too far away," or something stupid like that and I'd have been skunked. So I smother the shriek in my throat and ram down the rest of the cereal and the troll is coming along. She'll pay.

You have to understand. There are times when I really don't hate Nina. Like when she falls down and bleeds or some bully at school is picking on her or if she gets in bad trouble with my mother. But most of the time she's a giant pain and a gross liar and she borrows without asking and she never puts back, and if she does, it's always dirty and wrinkled, and she's sneaky and tends to rat on other people just to save her own skin. My general policy in regard to Nina is to consider the spot she's standing in— empty. It never works.

Anyway, she's coming to the station with us, and speaking of the devil, I think I hear the toad slithering into the kitchen now, ten minutes late already and naturally you have to add on seven minutes while my mother makes her wash her hands and face. Now I ask you, who in Penn Station is going to inspect her hands and face?

But at least we're on the move. I do a last-minute check of my suitcase to make sure I've got Liz's present, my English hairbrush, and some sensational new aqua eyeliner Steffie and I found in the ladies' room at Schrafft's. (Did you ever taste their fantastic hot fudge? Far out!)

"Who walks Norman?" my mother asks.

"She does! She does!" Nina shouts, jumping up and down like some kind of a nut.

"I already did, Mommy, so tell her to mind her own business." Of course my mother doesn't tell her. She never does anything I want.

We take a cab to Penn Station and Nina doesn't even look up from her love comic all the way there. Beats me why she's so hot to go with us.

While my mother is buying my ticket, I put the touch on Nina. She hoards her money and always has a ton of it. All I want to borrow is five dollars, but when it comes to money she's a miser. I can usually get anything out of her but money. I already know how I'm going to swing it. She's wearing my Argyle socks.

"Take off my socks," I tell her when she says no to the loan. "You said I could borrow them," she says. "That was two days ago," I remind her. "You were supposed to wash them out and return them yesterday." She puts her nose back into her love comic like I'm not even there. I

pull the comic away. "Take off my socks." I have to
work fast before my mother comes back. I know she's not
going to let me take the socks back now. Nina knows that
too, so she starts to take them off slowly, looking around
for my mother. She's balancing on one foot, and all I have
to do is poke my finger into that skinny ugly chest and
down she goes. It's so tempting, but I know she'll howl.
Still, it's worth it. I know she's never going to lend me the
lousy money so I pretend I'm reaching for the sock and
give her a little tap and whoops . . . there she sprawls.

"I'm telling . . . Ma!" She howls and it's almost all
one word. I can see my mother rushing over, ticket in
hand. "You're like two babies," she says for everyone to
hear. "I can't leave you alone for two minutes blah blah
blah . . ." She goes on in the mother voice with the
mother words. Nina is crying that I pushed her. I try to
explain in a calm voice that I only bumped her by accident
reaching for my favorite socks which she borrowed without asking, and, anyway, I want them back right now.

I admit it's all pretty stupid, but I'm not too far into it
now to pull out. My mother threatens to return the ticket
and call off the whole trip unless we stop "this very
instant." That's not fair. Naturally I'm going to stop, but
Nina's not going anywhere so she has nothing to lose, and
just to get at me, she keeps crying and pulling at the socks.

"Give her back the comic book," says my mother. I
toss it at the gnome just hard enough so it shoots past her
and lands on the floor. Big mistake. Not throwing it, but
letting her see that I'm wearing her charm bracelet.

Too late. "That's my bracelet!" She's practically
shrieking. The whole scene is getting very embarrassing
because people are stopping to stare at us and by now Nina
is even more disgusting than usual with her wet dirt-

streaked face and one bare foot. "She took it out of my drawer. Make her give it back right now."

I wish my train were pulling into the station so I could push her under it. Crunch. It would be worth losing a good pair of Argyles.

Nina is still making wounded-buffalo sounds and by now my mother is furious. "I don't want to hear one more word from either of you! Nina, put those socks on right this minute and meet us over there," she says, pointing to a big round information booth in the center of one wall of the station. We both walk toward it, leaving the sniveling creep sitting on the floor pulling on my socks.

"You call us Sunday afternoon and tell us what train you're making," my mother says to me, checking the clock over the booth with her watch. It's only a quarter to nine and my train doesn't leave for fifteen minutes so unfortunately there's plenty of time for instructions. "Either Daddy or I will pick you up on Sunday night, right here in front of the information booth. Now look around and make sure you know where we are." And my mother begins to point out things to help me remember where this one and only information booth right in the middle of two enormous marble pillars is. She's too much. I stop listening when she starts to show me how its directly under this monster Dupont Cinerama-type advertisement right opposite the escalator. It's not even worth reminding her that I've made this same trip twice in the last year and that they always pick me up in the same spot and that I'm really not a moron or a two-year-old.

By now the troll has joined us and she's ready for action.

"Mommy," Nina says, "tell her to give me my bracelet back. Ma . . ." Nina is the greatest whiner in the country. She has this special way of just letting her mouth hang down and making all the words seem to come directly out of her nose. My mother really hates it when she does that. You can tell by the glare on her face. I love it when Nina is on the other end of that look.

"I don't want to hear another word about socks or bracelets. How many times do I have to tell you, don't lend and don't borrow. You hear me? Now come on. Move." And she leads the way to Track 13.

I can't resist a tiny grin to aggravate Nina. "Maa . . ." she whines, pulling my mother's arm. "She's looking at me." But my mother's had it and she doesn't even turn around. There are some last-minute moronic instructions and then its time for good-bye kisses. For my mother only. I'm just about to hop up the steps when Nina, who's probably been busy plotting something horrible since upstairs, announces, "I need my bracelet for Emily's party Saturday afternoon."

Last week we had the word "smug" on a vocabulary test. Right now it's on my sister's face. I figure the best thing to do is pretend I didn't hear her and jump on the train. Before I can, she grabs my jacket and screams, and I mean screams, "I need my bracelet!" We're obviously everyone's free afternoon entertainment.

My mother says, "Give her the bracelet." I say I want my socks.

Sometimes in the middle of these arguments I think that I must have gone through the same fight billions of times with only one change. Sometimes it's socks, shirts, gloves, or hats. The fight's the same, only the item is different. It's getting late now and everyone else is on the train and I'm starting to get nervous. But there's no stopping now, so we go around again. Nina says she wants her bracelet, my mother says give it to her, and I say not until she gives me my socks. Now my mother is really furious and grabs the bracelet off my wrist and says, "I said give it to her."

It's all so stupid, I don't know why I do it, but I make a grab for the bracelet. I know it's a dumb move but I'm angry because it's really unfair. My mother's temper is gone and she smacks my hand.

"Get on that goddam train right this minute!" she screams at me.

I can see the people looking at us from the train windows. The tears make me practically blind and I can hardly see to grab my suitcase. I trip up the steps to the train. She shouts something else to me but I don't even hear her. I push through the door into the car, where everyone turns to look at me. The tears are rolling over my cheeks as I start down the aisle. Awful luck, the only empty seat is way down at the other end of the car. That means I have to walk past all these nosy people ogling at me. I don't even care any more. All I can think of is that my mother is the most unfair person in the whole world and I really think she's a *B-I-T-C-H* and I can't stand living with her any more. I'm not kidding, I'm really thinking of moving out. I'm steaming mad. I hate my mother and she's ruining my life. I hate her. Hate, hate, hate.

# *Three*

I have two things to say about the party in Philadelphia (I'm on the train home now). One, it started bad. Two, it got worse. In fact, the whole weekend bombed out for me, including Liz. I'm not in her house ten minutes when she breaks the news that she's not going to wear pants to the party after all. Instead, she's going to wear this gorgeous-looking silk dress. That's bad enough but I really start freaking out when she tells me that all the other girls are wearing dresses, too. Naturally I don't have one with me. And then she swears that she told me on the phone last week that it was dresses, but she's full of it because that's something a person doesn't forget. Maybe a school assignment could slip your mind but not what everybody's wearing to practically the most important party all term.

It wouldn't be so tragic if I could borrow something from Liz, but she's almost three inches taller than me so there I am, stuck wearing my sailor pants and feeling like a real jerk. Wait, it gets worse. Here it is Saturday night and I just looked in the mirror for a last-minute check. I know for sure my skin was super-perfect an hour ago, but now there is the biggest, grossest, most horrendous pimple in the history of the world growing smack out of the middle of my chin. Great! Now I'm really going to wow that David. The only five-foot-four-inch pimple dressed in pants and all his.

It turned out that I didn't have to worry about David after all. That's right. He never showed up for the party. No phone call or anything. Just another one of my long line of admirers. I really knock 'em out.

The party was a real downer for me anyway. I spent the whole evening sitting on the back porch talking to Annie Gordon, the fat girl from next door who Liz has to invite to all her parties. But that's not even the worst.

Two of the boys who think they're really hotshots lit up a joint right behind us on the porch and start puffing away like mad. Then Liz comes out and she gets right into the action. It hits me that she's being kind of dumb, I mean doing it practically right under her parents' noses, but I figure she knows what she's doing, so I keep quiet. Then she sees Annie and me and whispers, "Move closer and I'll give you a drag."

Annie's jaw falls a mile. She leaps up and takes off, clopping down the steps so fast she misses practically half of them. Actually it's a hysterical sight except instead of cracking up I probably should have followed her. But you know me, I have to be Miss Cool, so instead I just slide over and join the group. Fatal mistake.

I probably sound like I'm uptight about grass but I'm absolutely not. It's no big deal anymore. I mean, I hardly know anyone, except maybe Annie Gordon, who hasn't tried pot at least once. First time I smoked it was at this big fountain in Central Park where a whole load of kids hang out. They do it right out in the open. Anyway, I took a couple of puffs and it was okay, not outrageous like some kids say, but good enough. Still I don't think it's worth taking a big risk for, like at Liz's party, smoking on the back porch while her parents are right inside the house.

I'm up to my eyeballs in trouble already, so when Liz hands me the joint I tell her, "No, thanks, I'll pass this time."

You should have seen the way those weirdos look at me. Like I'm some kind of freak or something. Then the really gross one sitting next to me pipes up with, "Another Annie Gordon." And they all yak their heads of.

It's really hard not to let creeps like that get to you. I try—for almost ten seconds. Then I can't stand it anymore so I reach out, grab the stupid joint, take a giant drag, and let the smoke out right in Big Mouth's face.

"Perfect . . ." I say.

"Yeah," he says, real pleased.

". . . for my nine-year-old sister." I zing it to him. "What nursery school did you get this banana peel at?" And before he can stop stuttering I launch into two and a half minutes on the advantages of Acapulco Gold over Panama Red (or is it Acapulco Red and Panama Gold?). Somewhere in the middle of my brilliant dissertation three things happen: Liz reaches out for the joint, I start to hand it to her, and dear Aunt Hilda comes out of the house. I'm not saying I'm wonderful or anything, but even though I have just enough time to drop the butt into Liz's hungry little fingers, I keep the joint myself. I figure how can I stick her with it right in front of her own mother?

Aunt Hilda is pretty easygoing most of the time, but when she sees me holding that tiny wrinkled-up joint she knows right away what it is and lets out this little shriek and that's it. End of party. End of weekend. End of me. She starts sweeping everybody out of the house, and Liz goes right up the spout, crying and bawling and arguing with Aunt Hilda, but it does no good. The party's over.

Of course there's absolutely no way to convince her that it wasn't all my fault when she sees me sitting there with the joint in my hand, so I don't even try. Anyway, it's just like I said about how a hundred people can be doing something wrong and I'm the one who gets caught.

This time my aunt is angry at Liz too. But get this, only because she was "careless enough to allow Victoria to bring pot to the party."

It really freaks me out that Liz didn't even take part of the blame. Worse. She was actually teed off at me for getting caught. All she wanted to know was how come I didn't shove it in my pocket or step on it or eat it or something. Isn't that too much?

Then my Aunt Hilda says that it would be better if I went home because she couldn't let a thing as serious as "smoking a pot" (that's what she actually said. Good thing the guys weren't smoking two pots or she'd have called the police) go by without teaching Liz a very serious lesson. So to punish Liz, she sends me home. Neat logic, huh? And of course she has to call my mother Sunday morning and tell her the whole story. Right during breakfast. They talk for about a minute, then Aunt Hilda calls me to the phone. "I think your mother wants to say a few words to you."

"Mommy?" I ask, hoping for a dead connection.

No luck.

"This is the last straw . . . I've absolutely had it with you . . . This time you've gone too far . . ."

"But it wasn't my fault. I didn't bring the pot."

"I don't want to hear another word about it."

"I only took one drag. I didn't start it."

"Of course not, you never do!"

"But I'm not lying. I swear."

"I'm not going to argue over the phone. We'll discuss it when you come home."

"But I didn't—"

"I said we'll discuss it when you come home. There's a nine-forty-five. I want you to be on it."

"Shit."

"What did you say!"

"Nothing."

"What?"

"I said, I said nothing."

"Put Aunt Hilda back on."

Now my mother goes through a whole long thing with my aunt and my aunt keeps shaking her head "tsk tsk tsk" and looking at me. You know how you always read about somebody's stomach sinking? Well, that's mine now. I know I'll never be able to talk my parents out of sending me away to that gross boarding school now. I'm horrendously depressed at the thought of having to spend the next four years in P. S. Prison or whatever they call that disgusting place. Home may not be the greatest place in the world but it has to be better than reform school.

And all that garbage they're going to give me about how it's for my own benefit is just so much baloney. All they want to do is get rid of me and I know it. Do you know how it feels when your own mother and father don't want you? It's the worst thing in the world, that's what.

Rather than stand here and cry I start to get busy putting the dishes in the dishwasher.

"That's okay, Victoria, just leave them," says my aunt, putting down the phone. "You'd better get packed if you're going to make the nine-forty-five. I'll get my car keys and be ready in five minutes."

I go upstairs and throw my things in the suitcase and I'm back down in less than two minutes. My marvelous, adorable cousin doesn't say a word. She just keeps eating her waffle. Boy, was I wrong about her.

The train was in the station when we got there so we

really had to make a run for it. When it was time for
good-byes my aunt kissed my cheek but I didn't kiss back.
I was really pissed off at her. By the time I got to my seat,
we were moving. I flopped down without even looking out
the window and here I am. Miserable. What a mess. I
don't think I'll ever visit them again.

"I promise you, young lady, nothing's that bad." I look
up and see that it's the conductor leaning over me. He
happens to be wrong. It's very bad, but he's sort of an old
man with a nice pink face so I give him a smile while I
reach into my jeans for the ticket.

"That's better, Smiley," he says, bending his whole
face up into a big crinkly grin. We're practically nose to
nose and it's so silly that I smile for real.

As long as I've got the smile handy, I turn it toward the
old lady sitting next to me, and she likes it so much she
offers to change seats with me and let me sit near the
window. I love window seats. I must have had a million
arguments with my sister over who gets the window seat.
It's the difference between a boring hour and a half and a
fascinating experience staring out the window and getting
lost in somebody else's world. I really need to get lost
someplace today.

"Is this your first trip to New York, dear?" the old lady
wants to know. I tell her I live in New York and about my
cousin in Philly. Then she says that the first time she made
this trip was just before her daughter was born. I really
don't feel like talking so I don't listen too closely. I hope
she'll get the idea. I would love to say, "Please leave me
alone," or just not answer, but I'd never have the nerve so
I just keep shaking my head and pretend to be interested.

"Joseph, that's my husband, was truly upset with me
but I said to him, 'I'm the one who's having the baby and
I simply couldn't be comfortable unless I used Dr. Tuller

in New York.' After all, Ethel and I, that's my twin sister, had always used Dr. Tuller and I wasn't about to change now, what with a first baby and all. It took some fancy convincing but I finally said to him, 'When *you* have a baby you can use any Philadelphia doctor you want.' ''

This seems to strike her as positively hysterical. Too much. I start to laugh too, but not at her doctor story. I've got this wild picture in my head of another little old lady, the spitting image of this one. I wonder if they still dress alike. That would really be far out. Two twin old ladies with the same kerchief, lipstick and pointy patent-leather shoes all in shocking crimson. I'd love to ask her but she'd probably think I was being fresh. I am.

Luckily she gives up on me and goes back to her book. That gives me about ninety undisturbed minutes to sit here and work myself up into a panic about what my parents are going to do when I get home. Too bad worrying isn't a subject in school, I'd get straight A's. I'm the best around. If I cut myself, I'm sure I'm going to get lockjaw. If my parents argue, I worry they're going to get a divorce, and if they get sick, I'm sure they're going to die. I worry about being adopted (I'm not), failing tests, getting shots, robbers when I'm alone in the house, and spiders all the time, even when everybody's home.

No matter what the worry, it always feels the same. It's like somebody opened a louvered door in my stomach and let in a whoosh of icy wind that practically takes my breath away. And if that's not bad enough, there's a little metal ball that just sits way down in the pit of my stomach. It never moves, but it weighs a ton. As soon as I start to think about my mother's face when she meets me at the station I get all those old symptoms. I really dread that look of anger and disappointment.

My mother always says I look for trouble, but I really

don't. Just the opposite. In fact, trouble with anyone, particularly my mother, makes me miserable. I don't remember having problems with her when I was little. In fact, everything was just great then. I think it began to change when I got to be about twelve. We just never seemed to agree on anything after that. We even had an argument on my birthday last year. I don't remember, but it was probably something she wouldn't let me do. I know I've said I hate my mother, but I really don't. It's just that she seems a million miles away from me.

My elbows are probably filthy from leaning on the windowsill and my forehead's going to have a big black smudge from pressing against the pane, but that's my favorite position for train travel. I can just sit like that for hours watching the scenery shoot by. Seems like the whole trip to New York is nothing but miles and miles of split-level houses. Still, I'm not bored. I have a special thing that I do. I pick a house and concentrate on one tiny thing about it. Maybe the way a branch brushes against a window or some missing bricks on the side of the steps, something private that only the people who live in the house would know about. It's kind of like sneaking into their lives for a minute without their knowing it. It tickles me to think that I'm the only person in the whole world looking at the broken window shade on the house that just whizzed by. Then I always think, maybe it doesn't really exist—not just the window shade, the house and all of it. Maybe I made it all up. I remember one time my parents were having a discussion with some of their friends about different philosophical explanations of life and someone described Aristotle's, and it was just like that. I loved it. He said that you were the only real thing that existed in the world and everything else was a creation of your imagination, and if you weren't there, the world was empty.

Like now, all those houses, the people on the train, even the train itself is right out of my mind. I made them all up, including Aristotle and his ideas, and of course, if that's the case, I'm the only one alive and I get to live forever. Cool, huh? It could be possible, except the way I am with science I don't think I could really invent something as complicated as, say, electricity. On the other hand, I certainly could come up with a simple thing like a plug, which is all I ever get to see anyway. No wonder electricity is so mysterious—there's nothing on the other side of the wall. Just like a movie set, it's only what's in front of me that's real. Of course, the whole theory collapses when it comes to my mother. With any kind of person to choose from, why in the world would I stick myself with her? Another thought: if I know my mother, most likely *she's* real and I'm just a figment of *her* imagination. Obviously, Aristotle was off his nut and there really is something behind that plug on the wall, and with my luck I'm going to have to explain it all on some science test one day.

Suddenly I close my eyes, overcome by a terrible dread. I'm on a train heading home, where I'll never be able to explain away the pot business, and where they're bound to kick me out of school. As sure as I'm sitting here, my folks will send me off to that disgusting boarding school. I don't want to go home. I can't go home. I squeeze my eyes tight and try to will the train to stop. Come on, Aristotle or somebody. Help me. Where are all those great big mysterious forces floating free out there in the galaxies someplace? How do you get the train to stop? How do you get time to stop? If I could only stop time I'd be safe. Or better, make time go back a little so I'd have a chance to avoid the stupid things that got me in all this bad trouble in the first place. No cigarette up in the balcony. No party in Philadelphia. I'd even be nice to Nina.

Go back, train. Go back, time. Come on, give me a hand. I listen to the rattle of the train as it speeds through the countryside and I feel it's trying to help me. Clickety-clack, back and back. Clickety-clack, back and back and back and back. I lean forward to look out the window and see if maybe the crazy train isn't in fact going backwards, and just as I do the train makes one of those wild sways as it's rounding a turn and my head whacks into the window-pane. It's a good hard bang because there's an instant roar of thunder inside my skull and what feels like a bolt of lightning shooting down the back of my neck and into my spine. Pain. And in the next breath, gone. I'm okay, just a little shaky. Boy, you'd think they'd be more careful on those sharp turns. Even the train lights went out. And we must have hit the tunnel into Penn Station because it's black outside, too.

# *Four*

Now the lights in the train flash back on and I look around the car and everything looks calm. I guess I was the only one that got bumped. It must have been the way I was leaning on my elbows.

Wow! I didn't think ninety minutes could zoom by so quickly. It's only about five minutes from when you go under the tunnel until you get into Penn Station. The idea of going home to face all the trouble I'm in really freaks me out. Ugh. I dread it.

I excuse myself to the young woman sitting next to me and squeeze by her so I can reach for my suitcase over the seat. I'm especially careful because she's very pregnant. Funny, I never noticed when the old lady, the one with the twin sister, left and this young woman got on. I guess I was too busy with Aristotle. Even though I push as far as I can toward the seat in front when I inch past her, I manage to catch her toes under my wooden clogs. She jumps and lets out a loud "Ouch!"

"I'm really sorry," I say, but I have to look away because I'm in danger of breaking up at the sight of her struggling to reach her foot past that gigantic stomach. When she finally succeeds, she takes off the shiniest red pointy shoes you've ever seen, and rubs her toes. Her shoes look like something right out of *The Wizard of Oz*, but funny thing is, I could swear the old lady was wearing the same kind. They certainly look like old lady's shoes, even the wild color. Actually, the pregnant lady's taste is just about as awful as the old lady's with her matching scarf and crazy shoes and, oh my God, crimson lipstick. Bad taste must be catching.

Everyone is moving around, getting their luggage and making last-minute adjustments. The train slows down to a crawl as we enter the station.

I get a flash thought. Maybe I'll hide and stay on the train until we hit the freight yards and then I'll hook up with some hoboes and never go home. There's one small problem. I'm terrified of railroad tracks. It takes me forever to get up the courage to cross them. One of my big nightmares is that I won't know which is the third rail. I know some trains don't even use them, but I can never remember which ones. Science is just not my field, and neither, for that matter, are messy old hoboes.

Nothing to do but start making my way down the aisle to the door. It's slow moving because the car is packed with kids and mothers carrying babies. I must have been very wrapped up in my own problems 'cause I never even noticed all these babies. And, funny thing, I don't even remember hearing them. Though they sure are noisy enough now.

The pregnant lady is ahead of me and still limping a bit, but she turns and smiles at me, so I guess everything is all right. Everybody's shuffling along an inch at a time but that's okay with me. I'm certainly not in any big hurry to get to what's waiting for me. When I reach the end of the car, the conductor is helping one of the women. She's weighted down with a yowling baby, an old cardboard suitcase and a big hatbox from some store called "Wanamaker's." He's giving her a hand down the steps when he notices me. I get the same kind of huge happy smile as I did from the other conductor. I guess I never realized how warm and pleasant conductors could be. At least these two are. They must really like their jobs. It's easy to smile back.

"What'd I tell you, Smiley, nothing's that bad," he says, taking my elbow as I jump down the last step. When I hear him call me Smiley, I have to take another look to make sure it's not the original conductor. Of course it's not. This man can't be more than twenty-five, and the first conductor was at least sixty, but they do smile alike. Maybe they're father and son. If it wasn't so noisy and crowded I'd ask, but by now I'm already on the platform and being shoved along toward the steps at the far end.

Meanwhile another train has pulled in on the opposite side of the platform and people are pouring out and heading for the same steps. I'm snuggled deep inside the moving crowd, just letting myself be carried along. It might be nice to keep going with them and see where I end up. It's got to be better than in front of my mother.

On second thought, as I look around at the people, it might be a mistake. They're a very strange-looking group. You can tell they're really squares. All the women are wearing skirts and the men are dressed in baggy suits and most of them are wearing old-fashioned felt hats. Not even the kids are wearing jeans. In fact, nobody is but me. It's unreal. This has got to be some kind of convention group from Missouri or someplace. Something real snappy like librarians, funeral directors, and Eagle Scouts.

Just as I get to the steps I see this girl I know way back in the crowd.

"Hey!" I wave to her over the tops of some little kids.

She sees me and for a second looks kind of confused, like she's not sure I'm waving at her. But when I motion,

"Yes, you," with my head, she smiles and starts to make her way toward me.

Big mistake. When I look more closely, I see that I absolutely don't know her. Actually, she looks very familiar, but now that she's almost up to me I can see that I've never laid eyes on her before in my life. Bummer.

"Hi," she says right there in front of me, looking sort of blank but expectant.

Nothing to do but apologize. "Sorry," I say, "I really thought I knew you. I mean . . . it's incredible the way you look so familiar. . . . I could have sworn . . ." Mumble, stutter, stumble.

"That's okay, I guess I just have one of those familiar faces." And she smiles wider and I like her right off. "I'm Cici," she says. It's crazy but she really reminds me of someone I know. I mean absolutely.

"I'm Victoria," I say, and we both stand there like jerks. Only way out is to let ourselves go with the crowd, which we both do.

"See you around," she says, and she's gone. What an embarrassment.

We all march up the steps like in an orderly school fire drill, only nobody's pushing or shoving. I thought I came up the staircase that leads to the escalator, but I guess I was wrong. There's nothing here but another steep flight of steps. I'm probably dumb for sticking with this crowd. It's certain they've never been to New York before.

Sure enough, I'm lost. I've followed these hayseeds up some back stairs and ended up in a section of the station I've never seen before. Super! After going to Philly seven times, I get myself lost. Boy, my mother will never buy that one.

It's absolutely amazing that I've never seen this section of the station before. I mean, it's enormous. I don't see how I could have missed it. And it's jammed with people. Oh, gross! I bet I got off at the wrong station.

"Excuse. me, sir, can you tell me what station this is?" I ask a man in a sort of uniform with a red hat who looks like he must work for the railroad. He stares at me for a minute like he's trying to figure out if I'm pulling his leg, then decides I'm serious. "Pennsylvania Station, New York, New York." He booms it out like a conductor and then starts to laugh. "Where'd you think, girlie?" Embarrassing jerk. I don't think it's so funny and I'm about to tell him when somebody shoves a suitcase in his hand and he hurries off, not even waiting for my answer.

I'm being very calm despite the fact that when I look up at the towering ceiling and at all the gigantic space around me I get an awful scary feeling that something's really gone screwy. Maybe the man in the red hat is wrong. I ask a kindly-looking elderly woman and she gives me the same "are-you-kidding" look and then the same answer. Only she seems a little more concerned and I back off and lose her fast.

I'm looking around at this place and the people, and it's all really weird and at the same time—I don't know—kind of ordinary. Now it hits me! It's got to be. There's no other answer. I don't know why I didn't guess right away. Of course! They're shooting a movie! It's a cast of thousands and I'm stuck right smack in the middle. Super! I'm going to be in a movie.

To tell you the truth, I'm relieved. You remember those louvered doors I told you about in my stomach? The icy air, the metal ball, the whole bit? Well, it was beginning to happen. I'm not that hot to be in a movie, but I'm just out-of-my-head-happy that it isn't what I thought it was, which is very peculiar because I really don't even know what I thought it was. Though I probably won't be all that delighted when I see myself on the screen with my messy hair and the scaredy-cat look on my face. Ugh, I've probably got a dirt moustache where I wiped the sweat off my lip. And, as always, the twinkling tinsel teeth. At least I'll be able to pick myself out easily.

It's amazing the money they spend on these movie sets. They practically have to rebuild the whole station—well, the inside anyway. Will you look what they did to the information booth. It's half the size. You know, I can see how they can make something bigger, maybe add a cardboard wall here or there, or whatever, but I just don't know how they make an information booth smaller. And then if they did figure out how to shrink it, it would still have my mother in front of it. That tiny draft I get in my stomach is turning into a hurricane. Victoria, I tell myself, trying to sound strong like my mother, cool it. But I know it's only me telling me, so it doesn't work. Now I'm having trouble swallowing.

She could be late—my mother, I mean—or maybe the crowds are in the way or something. Just in case, I stand right in the center of the front of the information booth. On my toes with my arms up so she can't miss me. Right now, to tell the truth, I'm dying to see my mother. Even if she's angry. Nina would look pretty good to me now too, so you can imagine my state of mind. But so far no familiar faces.

Except one. Or, to be more exact . . . two. I may be freaking out, but remember the pregnant lady, the one with the pointy red shoes whose toes I squashed? Well, there she is, standing not ten feet away from me. Which is no big deal except that, at this very minute she happens to be hugging her identical twin sister. Well, think about it. That's a very weird coincidence—I mean, it must be a one-in-a-million shot for this pregnant woman to be wearing the same shoes, scarf, and crazy lipstick color and also have a twin sister exactly like the old lady who disappeared (well, *I* never saw her get off the train). I think that's pretty far out. In fact, it's so far out that my hands are shaking like some kind of weirdo. I shove them in my jeans pockets so nobody will notice. This is getting very heavy.

# Five

"Victoria?" The voice comes from behind me, but when I turn to look, I don't see anyone. I mean anyone I know. Then way back in the crowd I see an arm waving at me. From where I'm standing I can't see the person attached to it, but I'm feeling much better already because the arm is definitely waving at me and someone's calling my name. Wow! I was really getting worried. I can feel one of those goofy ear-to-ear grins spreading over my face as I watch the waving arm make its way through the crowd.

Forget it. Another bummer. It's only the girl from the train platform, the one I thought I knew.

"Hi." She's got a great smile, wide, white, and wireless. "Waiting for someone?" she asks.

"Yes, my parents. Well, my mother anyway. Except she's really late, which isn't like her at all."

"I thought you looked kind of worried. Why don't you give them a call?"

"I don't want to leave this spot in case she comes."

"You go call and I'll wait here. What's she look like?"

"I don't know, sort of ordinary, blondish hair, medium height. She'll probably be wearing jeans and a T-shirt."

"Blue jeans?" She looks really surprised.

"She lives in them."

"Well, that ought to make her pretty easy to find.

Okay, don't worry, I'll hold her here if she comes." I feel better already to have someone else involved. "The phones are way over there," she says pointing across the huge waiting room.

I head for the phones without looking too hard at the people because they just make me nervous. I put in two nickels and start to dial. Right away one of my nickels comes back. I let the phone ring forever but there's no answer. I try again and the same thing happens with the nickels but there's still no answer. She must be on her way. I head back to the information booth.

Cici is still waiting in front.

"There's no answer so they must be on their way here."

We stand around for about ten minutes, not doing much talking, just looking around. I think I spot my mother's head, hair, arm, what have you, half a dozen times. But I turn out to be wrong every time. I must be getting jumpy.

"Why don't you try to call them again? I'll wait here." I'm fantastically lucky to have run into Cici. I'd really hate to be alone at a time like this.

It turns out we wait for more than an hour. I call eight more times and still no answer. Now I'm plenty worried. It's just not like my mother not to show. She's never even late.

"Look, Victoria, why don't you come home with me and we'll call from there."

"I don't know if I should. What if she comes after I leave? Then she'll really worry." And probably be mad, if I know her.

Still, it's not such a bad idea. Having her worry, I mean. Who knows, she might get so scared that I've run away or gotten kidnapped or something horrendous like that that she may have second thoughts about sending me away to boarding school. Like she could realize how terrible it is without me. Well, maybe that's a little much, but still, it certainly would give her a jolt and I wouldn't mind that. Why should I be the only one to suffer all the time?

"Okay," I say, "let's go. I'll call from your house." Wow! Are they going to freak out! I think I take Cici by surprise. She probably didn't expect me to agree so fast, but she looks delighted.

"Neato!" she says. "Let's hurry. I'm starving." By now Cici has gotten hold of my arm and is leading me through the crowd, and dopey me, I'm letting her. We go down two flights of steps and end up at the IND subway heading for Queens. I guess I should have asked where she lives and things like that, but now it's too late.

It looks like I'm stuck with her. It's not all that terrible because I can tell right off that I'm really going to like Cici. You know how it is, sometimes you just meet someone and bang, you hit it off. Better than that, you're old friends instantly.

We can hear the subway train pulling in as we get to the turnstiles. "Hold it a minute!" I say, and start rummaging through my pockets for two tokens I know I had.

"I've got it," Cici says, shoving what looks like two nickels into the turnstiles. "Quick! The train's here."

Crazy. The nickel things work and we both bolt through, zoom down the steps and into the train just as the doors begin to close. We're out of breath and laughing hard. She's too much. She wasn't even nervous using those slugs. I got to remember to ask her where she gets them.

We're in one of those real old trains with the woven straw seats. You hardly ever see them in Manhattan anymore. It's pretty crowded and there are no empty seats so we both grab different poles.

Now, for the first time, with Cici standing far enough away, I can get a real good look at my new friend. She's maybe an inch or two shorter than I am, not skinny but real slim and I'm happy to say even more flat-chested than me. Her hair hangs a little below her ears and she's got it parted on the side with a big dangly wave that keeps sliding across her right eye. I love it and you know what? It's exactly like that Veronica Lake thing I tried to do that my mother made me change. Shows you what she knows. Anyway, it's streaky blond and a little frizzy, sort of the way mine looks when I don't blow-dry it. I'd call her pretty, in fact, maybe even very pretty. Especially in the outfit she's wearing. She's got on one of those old-fashioned peasant skirts, the kind I'm always looking for—you know, gathered tight at the waist and swinging out real full down to the middle of her calves. Her blouse is great too, with puffed lacy sleeves and a scoop neck. Sometimes, if you're super-lucky, you can pick up things like that in a thrift shop. Like I said, her clothes are sensational, but you should see her shoes and socks. You wouldn't believe how gross they are. Her shoes look exactly like men's brown loafers, and to top it off she's wearing heavy white gym socks. And if that isn't horrendous enough, she's got shiny copper pennies stuck inside the front slot of each shoe. Ugh. I've got to tell her what a big mistake she's making. Maybe later, when we get to be better friends. Though actually, it feels like we're pretty good friends already. Like I said, sometimes it just happens that way.

Right now, standing here and staring at Cici, it's really beginning to bug me that she looks so familiar. I bet I know her from some place. Maybe summer camp. I go over to where she's standing and ask her if she's ever been to camp. She says she has and names three camps that I've heard somebody mention—I can't remember who—but when I try a few names on her—Judy Rubin, Cait Clancy, Jill Schwartz—she doesn't know them. And she's never heard of the camps I've gone to. Maybe I don't know her, but she absolutely reminds me of someone I do know and it's going to drive me batty till I remember who.

As I look around, it hits me that the people going to Queens look a lot like the people in Penn Station, who don't look much like the people I'm used to seeing every day. Which makes me think that either fashions change faster than I thought or the people in Queens are about thirty years behind the times. I guess you can see how hard I'm trying to squeeze everything into plain old ordinary explanations. I don't think it's working too well.

The train rumbles on with the lights blinking on and off every now and then. At one point in the darkness, cut off from Cici, a weird scary feeling comes over me that the car is really empty and I'm all alone. Not just here in the subway, but everywhere. It's sort of like that Aristotle thing again, except that when the lights come back on and I look around, I know all this couldn't be my creation. If it was, then I wouldn't feel so out-of-place—and I really do.

I can't explain why I'm freaking out now or why this all seems so weird. I mean, when you're riding on the subway to Queens, how far out can it be? That's just what makes it so bizarre, when something that should be so ordinary is so unusual. Take these people. They seem like plain old everyday New Yorkers—dressed up in costumes. Which is something even plain old everyday New Yorkers just don't do when they ride the subway.

Even the subway car is different. Very old-fashioned, as I mentioned, but also too clean. There's only one tiny bit of graffiti and it doesn't even make sense. It's a little picture of a guy's eyes and nose peeking over a line with the words, "Kilroy was here," underneath. No house number, no nothing. And the advertisements. I've never even heard of half of them. What's Citronella? Where's Luna Park? And now that I take a good look around, Cici isn't the only girl in those awful shoes.

The train pulls into Ely Avenue and some people get off. Cici pokes me and points to two empty seats. We sit down and she takes some grimy piece of grayish-white material out of her pocketbook. It's all rolled up in this disgusting ball held closed by a needle with some gray thread. She unravels a tiny corner and starts to sew with the most grotesque stitches you've ever seen. Beats me what that rag could be and why anyone would bother sewing such a thing. I'm about to ask about it, but I catch myself at the last second and instead ask what stop we get off at.

"We gotta go to the end of the line," she says. "Parsons Boulevard. Are you hungry? I'm starving."

I'd forgotten to even think about food, but now that I do, I guess I'm kind of hungry too. "Yeah," I say, "I could eat."

"Terrif," she says. I notice that she uses that word a lot. "We can grab a chow mein sandwich at Woolworth's."

Gross me out! I love Chinese food, but a chow mein sandwich on white bread toast probably, with lettuce and a pickle sounds horrific, but I don't want to hurt her feelings so I pretend I'd love one.

"Your skirt is a groove," I tell Cici. "I love it. I've been looking for one like that forever. Where'd you get it?"

"My mother got it for me."

"I bet she picked it up in a thrift shop." Somehow mentioning a thrift shop was a mistake because she looks at me really funny, like either I'm kidding or I'm nuts. For a second she even looks kind of insulted, so I smile to show her I didn't mean anything bad, then she laughs and says, "Yeah."

Something tells me to drop the subject and I do.

An old man sitting next to us beckons with his finger for us to lean over and look at something in his hand. Naturally I pay no attention. All my parents have to find out is that I was talking to some strange man in the subway . . . beautiful. I'd never hear the end of it. Cici surprises me though. She smiles and bends over to look. I think she must be nuts. In fact, I wish she wouldn't do it because I always get a little nervous in the subway anyhow, with all those rapes and knifings, I mean. I poke Cici and shake my head, "no," but she doesn't seem to get the message. Now she really looks interested in what he's showing her and pulls me over to have a look. I can't believe how she's not even the least bit nervous about this man.

She's got me hanging over him so I can't not look. Turns out he's trying to show us something on the inside of a peanut. Did you know that if you separate the two halves of a nut, inside is this thing that looks exactly like the face of Santa Claus? I never knew that before. He gives us each a nut. I put mine right in my pocket. You know I'm not about to eat food from a stranger. Though, strangely enough, this time I almost feel I could.

Weird, but when the old man showed us the nut thing, the other people around us seemed to lean closer and smile like they were approving. They even seemed friendly. Can you picture people in a subway being interested and friendly? And another thing, you probably think I'm exaggerating, but you know that feeling you get in the subway? Uptight, tense, like something horrendous could happen at any time? I don't feel it here. I actually feel very relaxed, like I couldn't be in a safer, more comfortable place. And if that old man tried anything funny on us, I get the feeling the other people would cool him fast. I must be dreaming.

Cici and I chatter away for the rest of the trip. We seem to have a million things in common. Especially problems. She tells me about how she's always getting into trouble for the littlest, most unimportant things. Just like me. Plus she hates the way she looks, too. I tell her she's crazy because she's really cute-looking, but she says her eyes are too small and close together and she thinks her knuckles are too big.

"But the worst things are my knees. Look." And she lifts her skirt enough to show me perfectly okay-looking knees, and believe me I'm an expert on knees so I know what I'm talking about.

"What's wrong with them?" I ask because maybe it's something I can't see.

"Are you kidding? They're so bony you could cut yourself just looking at them."

She's nuts. They're fine and there's nothing the matter with her eyes either. But I know she'd never believe me, so all I say is, "Wait till you see mine."

And then she tells me how she's a social flop with boys, and we compare all the jerky mistakes we've made at parties, and we're practically hysterical because we both do the same goofy things.

I think she's as excited about me as I am about her. She starts to tell me about all the great plans she's got for us today. First, we're going to eat at the five-and-dime, then a double feature (I told her I only have three dollars to spend; for some reason she thinks that's hysterical), then later, after dinner, a big party at some boy's house. I tell her it all sounds fantastic, and she says that as long as I love her outfit so much, I can borrow her other one which is much dressier and even nicer. Luckily her feet are

super-tiny, like a size one, so there's no question of me
borrowing her gross shoes. I tell her that I think my clogs
(would you believe she never even heard of clogs?) would
be perfect with the skirt. She doesn't say anything but I
can see that she thinks my clogs are as weird as I think her
loafers are.

Still, you can tell that things like what kind of shoes a
person wears don't matter to Cici. She's the easygoing
type that doesn't try to shove her opinions on you. That's
one of the things I like so much about her. You do what
you want and she does what she wants. Plenty of room for
everyone.

At Parsons Boulevard the train empties and we go up
the stairs and out of the subway. We stop in a candy store
and I try to phone my house. Still no answer. Cici says
that we have to walk a few blocks to the main drag,
Jamaica Avenue. Everything's there.

At Woolworth's the lunch turns out to be sensational. I
eat two gigantic chow mein sandwiches and they're nothing like I thought they'd be. It's a big blob of really great
chow mein served with a whole bunch of crispy fried
noodles on a soft hamburger bun and it's delicious. Plus—
you won't believe this—it only costs a dime.

I don't know much about the price of chow mein
sandwiches, but when the girl behind the counter asks for
a nickel for an orange drink, I nearly choke. And it's not
just what they charge for the food, it's everything—lipsticks,
hair junk, school stuff—it's all half the regular price. I
look around to see if it's a special sale day, but I don't see
any signs. I try to think of an easy explanation, but the
only plausible one I can come up with (and I admit it's
reaching a bit) is that I just wasn't paying attention again.
That's what my science teacher is always saying about me.
I dream.

Well, I must have been dreaming the day they explained all this. I mean this whole thing was probably planned in advance as a commemoration of some national event, and the day they told everyone, I just wasn't listening. I was probably dreaming or doodling or something like that, and now here I am stuck right smack in the middle and too embarrassed to ask. Serves me right, I guess.

The other explanation is a lot simpler. I've flipped my lid, gone bananas. All that science homework that Mr. Flynn gives could really make you crazy.

## Six

If either of those explanations don't really grab you, I've got another one. Only I can't exactly describe it because it's very far out, more vibes than something tangible. But there are three things I'm absolutely certain about. One, all this has nothing to do with any of my real problems (being suspended from school and being falsely and practically accused of dealing pot, which is really horrendously unfair). Two, it started way back there on the train. And three, it's real heavy stuff. I can tell because the vibes I'm getting are very negative. For a person who gets jumpy just going up in an elevator alone at night, this is freak-out stuff. So far I haven't—freaked out, I mean. But I think that's mainly because of Cici. She's solid and real and I trust her completely, and that's what keeps me calm, sane, cool. Meanwhile, I think I just saw my solid trustworthy friend take the old five-finger discount. That's shoplifting in case you didn't know. Though why she wants something that says "toggle bolts" on the package beats me. For that matter, what is a toggle bolt anyway?

"What did you do that for?" I whisper into her shoulder.

"What?" she says, all innocent.

"Snatch the funny-looking bolt."

"Oh," she says, really crushed, "you saw me take it?"

"Sure, you scooped it up in your sleeve."

"How about the eraser?"

"I missed that one."

"Aha! It worked. That's my new method. See, what I do is lick my palm and then press it down hard on the eraser and—presto!—it sticks to my hand, and then it's simple to slip it right into my pocket. Watch."

And she goes to work. With a great flourish, she licks her hand and jams it down against a small rubber electrical plug. *A hundred people turn to look.* Including the store manager. She's the worst thief I've ever seen. I try to make crazy motions to her so she doesn't put the plug in her pocket, but she's so carried away with her new method that she doesn't notice my frantic hand motions until it's too late. I never thought being collared meant the store manager comes over and actually grabs you by the collar. But that's exactly what happens to Cici and with me standing there like some kind of jerk not knowing what to do.

Meanwhile the manager goes into a long spiel about how he's going to call her parents, the police, her school, et cetera, and he's going to press charges, and with this black mark against her she'll never be able to go to college or hold a job or anything. After he goes on for about five minutes about how she's finished for life, he says to her, "And now, young lady, what do you have to say for yourself?"

And Cici turns to him and says, bold as brass, "Ohta foeks elitna meonmen ogla."

Right on! I think she may be the greatest girl I ever knew in my whole life.

"Mashconki," she says to me, "wahofa dorma conchi?"

I shrug my shoulders and answer, "Vaggon."

Now she turns back to the manager, who's looking very confused and gives him a huge Yugoslavian-type smile (whatever that is) and, reaching over to the counter, takes another of those indispensable rubber plugs and with the most heartbreaking of limps drags herself over to me and hands me the plug. Now, obviously in excruciating pain, she makes her way back to the speechless manager and with a hideously lopsided curtsy, mumbles to him, "Absarupa," and shakes his hand.

Taking my cue from her (but with only the courage for a small facial tic), I nod to the manager and also shake his hand and give him a hearty, "Absarupa."

It's all so successful that we turn to the crowd that has gathered and with a humble bow and our warmest smiles, wish them all an "Absarupa." I think I see tears in one old woman's eyes as they answer in unison, "Absarupa."

Hostilely they turn to the manager, who swallows his embarrassment, stuffs two more plugs into Cici's twisted hand, and gulps, "Absarupa."

Now, for the final touch, Cici contorts her head toward the audience, and with such effort that her whole body trembles, says, "Omerika goot!"

My stomach is beginning to turn, but the crowd applauds, and with one last (I hope) magnificent gesture, Cici hands each person a brown rubber plug. One thing I can tell about Cici already is that she doesn't know when to stop, so I allow her one last "Absarupa," grab her by her good arm, and shove her toward the exit. We move pretty fast, considering her afflictions.

A minor miracle strikes someplace between the lipstick counter and the front glass doors, and when we burst into the street, she's completely cured. Grabbing hands, we charge down the block, zip across the street and down the next block, yelping with laughter, gasping for breath. With a tug from Cici we go flying slam into the ticket booth of a movie theater. Still hysterical.

"You're crazy," I tell her between giggles and snorts. "I can't believe we got away with it. He must be some kind of a moron."

"I've got this terrific idea for when we go back later," says my lunatic friend. "I got this thing we can do with our jackets that'll make us look like Siamese twins. We both get into the same jacket. Here, all you do is . . ." And she starts to wiggle out of her jacket.

"Show me later," I say, pushing her jacket back on. "We'll miss the movie."

No question about it, I was right. Cici is sensational, but she definitely doesn't know when to stop. Never in my life will I enter that five-and-dime again. In fact, I may never go into any other Woolworth's anywhere. I start fishing into my pockets for my money.

"Did you see these pictures?" she asks, and out comes that rolled-up rag again as she digs into her pocketbook for money.

I study the movie posters. "No, but I think they were on TV."

"Huh?" she says, screwing up her forehead like she never heard of TV or something. "On what?"

There go those vibes again. "Nothing," I say. "They look super to me. Actually I've been dying to see them." It's not true, but it seems to satisfy Cici, and besides, something tells me it's better not to go into it now. Then I catch sight of the admission price. At first glance I think it says seventeen cents, then I realized that that must be the tax so I study it closer. It's really weird, but it's not the tax. That's the whole price. Seventeen cents to see *Laura* and *Since You Went Away*. Even if we are in Queens and they are old movies, still, that's the most incredible bargain I've ever heard of. At that price I can afford to be a sport, so I pay for both tickets.

"Hey!" Cici is delighted. "Thanks. That's terrif. I'll buy the candy."

We go in and it's one of those gigantic old theaters that look like a castle in fairyland. It's even got that funny kind of ceiling my mother used to tell me about. It's fixed up to twinkle. When my mother was little, her brother, my Uncle Steve, used to take her to scary movies and she'd spend the whole time staring up at the ceiling trying to figure out how they did it. If she didn't tell me that they run a movie of the sky on the ceiling, I would never know. It's so incredibly real-looking. I didn't think they had this stuff in theaters any more. Bet this is probably the last one left in the city.

We find two perfect seats right in the center aisle and start squeezing in past the people when suddenly someone flashes a big spotlight on us.

"Just a minute there, girls. Where do you think you're going?" It's a woman's voice. Cici grabs my arm and starts pulling me as fast as she can in the opposite direction, crunching toes, bumping knees, and tripping over people.

"Excuse me. Excuse me," we keep mumbling.

"Hey, watch it!"

"What d'ye think you're doing!" Everyone in the row is furious.

The flashing light circle is bounding over us. Whistles, applauding, and angry shouts come from the rest of the audience. Oh, God, it's like the class trip, only no Miss Fatso. Worse. I catch a glimpse of what looks like a nine-foot-tall Amazon in a white uniform right out of all those women's prison pictures. I don't even bother to look where I'm going, I just let Cici lead me.

We dash up the aisle and into the lobby and shoot behind a huge goldfish pond with a waterfall and a real goldfish the size of a flounder in it. We spot the monster prison matron coming up the aisle hot on our trail, red-faced, huffing, and furious. She goes right over to the next aisle and stands there waiting to catch us. Cici starts to wiggle out of her jacket. Oh, please, God, don't let it be that awful Siamese-twin thing.

Now I'm really shaking and I don't even know why. I didn't do anything wrong. I paid for the tickets. I think. Why is that monster chasing us? And why are we running? Now Cici starts to laugh. We're going to end up spending the whole double feature crouched behind the goldfish pond. Maybe that's why it's only seventeen cents.

"As soon as the witch goes down that aisle," she says, giggling and loving the whole thing, "we'll make a run for the end aisle." And she ties her jacket around her waist, the better to run with. Whew. At least it's not the twin jazz.

"Why?" I ask her. I mean this is really getting dumb, running and not knowing why.

"Because it's against the wall and she won't be able to see our outline."

"No," I say, "I mean why are we running?"

"So we don't have to sit in the children's section."

"The children's section! Gross! I'm almost fourteen. Why should I sit in the children's section?"

"Because that thing says so," she says, jerking her head toward the gargantuan matron. "She's in charge of the children's section, and she doesn't care how old you are. If she says you sit there, it's TS. You sit there. Now, are you ready to make a dash for the end aisle?"

"You bet. Nobody's putting me in any dumb children's section. By the way—what's TS?"

"You kidding? Tough Shit on her! Now!" And with the matron's back toward us, we shoot for the end aisle. A second before the aisle door, Cici stops dead.

"My dress! I left my dress behind the goldfish pond."

That ball of rags is a dress? Too much.

"Leave it," I say. "We'll get it later on our way out."

"No good. Somebody'll take it."

Not unless there's a garbage pickup. I'd really love to know who'd want that thing, but she seems so attached to it I can't ask.

"You want to wait here?" she says.

"Uh-uh." No, sir. I'm not about to take a chance on losing Cici. She may be my last friend in the world.

So we race back. Just as I thought, the dress is rolled up in a ball right where she left it. She's really relieved and jams it into her bag. Here we are again, back crouching behind the fish pond. By now I figure we've missed about one-third of the picture. Cici reads my thoughts. "Don't worry," she says. "I always sit through them twice anyway."

"Okay, now's our chance," Cici says, and we fly toward the end aisle. Just as we hit the door the matron comes out of the other aisle and spots us.

"Come back here this instant."

Oh, boy, four huge steps and she's halfway across the theater. We race through the door and into a wall of darkness. It takes a couple of seconds to be able to focus. I can hear the heavy thud of her feet behind us. Bummer! Wouldn't you know. I don't see any empty seats. Then, just as the light begins to crack through the door behind us, Cici spots two seats a couple of rows ahead. They're not together; one is on each side of a man. We lunge for them. Cici slides in past the man and I take the one closest to the aisle. Just as we thump down into our seats, the ominous flashlight comes bounding down the aisle, leaping up and down the rows searching for the escaped murderers.

I fight down the urge to slide down in my seat. The

littler I am, the more I'll look like a kid, so I sit up as tall
as I can. Maybe she'll think I'm the guy's wife. Now the
other people are beginning to give the matron nasty looks.
She's disturbing them. My idea works—she can't find us
so she has to retreat. I peek around and see her face in the
little window of the door. She's probably going to hang
out there waiting to trap us. Well, she's going to have a
long wait because we're not planning to move for a good
four hours.

I look across the man at Cici and we both smile. We
won! We outfoxed the dragon. Groovy! I slump back in
my seat feeling very up and ready to enjoy the movie. But
something begins to nag at me about the man sitting
between us. I think they call it peripheral vision when you
see something out of the corner of your eye that you don't
even know you're seeing. Well, most of the time you
don't notice unless something about it strikes you funny
like the fact that the guy is all huddled up in a raincoat
when it's as sunny as can be outside and it absolutely isn't
raining in the theater. Now, I'm no dope, so I know all
about men with raincoats, but I got my fingers crossed. He
could be the exception, you know.

Naturally I can't concentrate on the movie anymore. All
I'm doing is waiting for the inevitable. It happens. Or
maybe it doesn't happen. That's always the trouble with
these things. I could swear something touched my knee.
Of course it could have been the edge of his coat brushing
against me or it could have been his leg when he changed
position or it could have been something someone dropped
from the balcony or it could have been his goddam grungy
hand. Nothing I can do but sit and wait and see if it
happens again.

It happens again! This time there's no mistake. It's his
hand. It skims across my knee. Now, it could be acciden-

tal or it could be on goddam purpose. I'm beginning to perspire something awful. I even feel nauseous. I look behind me and sure enough, the matron's face is still framed in the window of the door. I don't even dare glance in Cici's direction because I have to look past the creep. I'll give him one more chance.

Big mistake. This time it doesn't just brush against me. It stays there. *There's a hand on my knee!* I'm frozen to the spot. Nothing moves on the outside, but inside my head it's all tearing around frantically. There's a hand on my knee! Gross! My eyes are staring so hard I think they're going to pop. Oh, God! I'm trapped between the dragon in the back and this disgusting goon. I want to slam his hand off me and scream, "Get away from me, you filthy old man!" I want to kick him with all my might right in the shin. I want to run out of this horrible theater. I want to go home!

"Get away from me, you filthy old man!" My God, did I say that? No . . . it's Cici and she's yelling at the top of her lungs, and everybody is turning to look, and now she winds up and gives him a bonebreaker kick right in the shin, and he jumps a mile and grabs his leg and lets out a long "Ooooooh . . ."

Believe it or not, I haven't moved a hair. Now Cici pushes past him and grabs my hand.

"Come on. This stinks." And turning to the man, who's still rubbing his leg, she says good and loud, "You disgusting pervert."

She really has guts.

Cici isn't finished yet. She pulls me out into the aisle, turns to the man, and shaking her finger just like my mother would do, really chews him out.

"You've got some nerve. I ought to call the police." Naturally nobody in our section is watching the movie anymore, but the rest of the audience is in a fury, whistling, stamping, and shouting for quiet. The old guy has slumped so far down into his seat that he's nothing but a pile of raincoat. Everyone around is grumbling at him and making hostile remarks. Finally he's so shamed that he leaps up and races out, knocking into the matron charging straight for us. There's no place to hide and the only place to run is the emergency exit. The matron or the movie?

We both make the same decision at the same second and shoot right out the door and into the back alley. Well, there goes thirty-four cents down the drain.

"I guess that wasn't such a good idea," Cici says, and she looks really upset. "Sorry you wasted all that money." Sometimes I can't tell whether she's serious or what. Just in case she's not kidding, I tell her it's okay, I'll catch them at home.

"Where?" She says it like I'm nuts.

"TV," I say.

"You mean TS."

"TS?"

"It sure is," she says, "on us."

Somewhere this conversation got away from me. But it doesn't make any difference because Cici is already half-way into another one and I can tell from the sparks that she's got a new plan. And it's going to be a beaut.

"I still got the other half of our tickets. Maybe I can talk to the guy at the door. I've got the perfect story. All I say is . . ."

Oh, no. I can't believe her. I'd rather go back to the manager at Woolworth's than mess with that matron. Cici really freaks me out, but I love her. I never had a friend who was nuttier or more exciting. She sure is different, except she's not. It's that weird familiarity thing again. Like right now she's gabbing on about her newest scheme and I'm not even listening. I'm just watching her expressions and the way she moves her hands and all, and thinking how she reminds me of someone I know. It's on the edge of my brain, but I can't grab it. And it's going to drive me loony.

". . . and if it doesn't work? So TS. It's worth the try. What do you think? Wanna try?"

I'm so involved in trying to figure out who she looks like that I miss half her plan, but that's okay because the part I did catch was all about some dread tropical disease and the life-saving medicine we supposedly left on the seat in the theater, and all I have to do is pretend I'm a blind nun.

"Sounds like a great idea, Cici." I try not to choke too loud. "But I'm really kind of beat and besides I'm getting tired of dragging this suitcase around. Would you mind if we passed it up for now?"

"Sure thing. Why don't we dump your things at my house and I'll save the stubs for tomorrow?"

Maybe I'll feel more like a blind nun tomorrow.

## Seven

We start walking down the alley toward the street. Of course, I have no idea where she lives so I just follow along. When we hit the end of the alley we turn right and we're on the main street again. This time we walk slowly and I get a chance to look around. First store I see is a National Shoe store. I study the window slowly and carefully. Last week I bought a pair of corkies in the one around my neighborhood for $14. This store obviously doesn't carry corkies, but they do have a whole lot of really gross shoes with little wedgies for prices all the way up to $2.99. That's right, two dollars and ninety-nine cents. For shoes. Not slippers—regular shoes. It's getting harder and harder to keep my cool.

We walk past other stores and it's the same story. All the prices are ridiculously low and the clothes are weird and the people are strange-looking and I'm running out of excuses.

I have to admit that I don't feel as freaked as I did at first. Maybe that's because I'm getting used to it or maybe it's Cici. She couldn't possibly be a part of anything that would hurt me. I just know it. I trust her. Absolutely. Besides, I've got at least two inches and ten pounds on her so she better not try anything funny. Okay, that's settled. Now all I have to do is get my head together and examine this whole thing calmly and rationally. Later I can get hysterical.

Right now I've got to be objective.

If this kind of thing happened to a character in a book I would say it's got to be science fiction, but since it's really happening to me, it's more like science nonfiction. That's a good start, isn't it? And another thing. I'm pretty sure that I'm not on another planet or anything far out like that. I mean everything is only slightly different . . . like an old movie.

I know it's not like the twenties because I just saw *The Great Gatsby* and nobody was dressed like this, and besides the cars and the clothes and everything look more like the ones in the beginning of that Barbra Streisand picture, *The Way We Were*. I think that was supposed to take place in the forties. Okay, so just say this is the forties. The forties! I must be out of my head, whacko. I mean, how come? How can I be in the forties, and if I am, what am I doing here and how am I ever going to get home and back to my family in the seventies?

Cool it, Victoria.

This kind of calm rational thinking can really make a person crazy. Still, I can't beat around the bush anymore. I've got to say it. So here goes.

I think some horrendously screwy thing has happened to me and I got zapped back in time. I know this sounds really far out, but just suppose somehow I fell into a time fault. You know like those faults they have in the earth in California. Well, maybe there's something like that in time and somehow I got sucked into one and zoomed back thirty years. My science teacher is always saying that nothing is ever wasted in nature, so maybe all those used-up years are still around someplace, sort of stored way down deep in the center of time. I guess I better level with you. I got a 32 on my last science exam. But just say I'm right. Then that's super. I mean I'm lucky because I could have fallen much farther, like thousands or even millions of years, and then there would have been dinosaurs or an ice age or something really gross like that.

Okay, so great, I only fell thirty years. Still, how am I going to get home? Or will I have to stay here always? Which is awful because except for Cici I'm absolutely alone here. In fact, it's even worse than that because I've got this outrageous secret and I can't even tell her. Just picture if I did. She'd probably think I was nuts or a liar or just trying to be cute and then she'd stop liking me and I couldn't bear that. I definitely can't let her know.

Another thing that's even scarier. I know you can fall down into something, but I'm not that lousy in science not to know you can't fall up. In other words, I could be stuck here for the rest of my life.

And if that's true, and it looks like it may be, I'm never going to see my mother and father again. Even Nina. I'll never have to look at that grungy face again. I can feel the tears coming already. Count to ten, jerk, think of your big toe, fine, now think of your little toes, whatever you do, don't cry! Think happy. Hey, no science term paper! No use. Here they come . . . ten, nine, eight, big toe, little toe. . . .

"Hey, what's the matter?" Cici's voice is very concerned.

I can't tell her the whole truth, but since she's my only friend, I have to tell her something. "I don't know," I say. "I just feel upset. Maybe it's because I had this really gross fight with my mother before I left and then when she wasn't there to meet me . . . Oh, I don't know, it's so depressing to fight with your mother, especially if you're not going to see her. . . ."

"It's better that way."

"Huh?"

"Sure. Gives her time to cool down. Mothers aren't so great, but they don't usually hold grudges. I know mine doesn't. That may be the best thing about her. Actually, she's probably a great mother—you know, cooking, cleaning, not letting you sit in a wet bathing suit and all that, but she's really tough—strict and very serious about being a mother."

"Mine too. I mean serious about being a mother. That's really our big problem. She can't understand me at all because it's like she was never a kid. Like she was born a mother."

"I know exactly what you mean. She probably drove her Dydee dolls crazy too. I've promised myself that when I have kids I'm really going to understand them because I'll remember what it was like for me."

I tell Cici that that's just the way I feel, and we congratulate ourselves on what sensational mothers we're going to make. And you know what? I'm beginning to feel better. Cici seems to have that effect on me. It's her kooky way of looking at things. She sort of tilts everything.

"I live right up this hill and in half a block." Cici interrupts my daydreams and points up a very steep hill.

I've been so involved in trying to get it all together that I didn't even realize we weren't on the main drag anymore. Now we're in sort of a residential area with mostly old wooden houses. Not really like suburbia, more like the city but with private homes, one jammed in right next to the other with little squiggly cement walks like you draw when you're a little kid. Everything looks very neat and clean. In fact, since that funny little Kilroy picture in the subway, I haven't seen one speck of graffiti anywhere.

We pass one of those old-fashioned candy stores and I tell Cici maybe I should try to phone my mother again.

"Sure," she says, "go on. I'll wait out here."

"I'll only be a sec," I say, and shoot inside, practically falling over the newspaper stand. A paper called *PM* slides down to the floor. Now's my chance. I bend down to pick it up and zero right in on the date. I gotta know if I'm . . . oh, wow! It says May 19, 1944. 1944! I can't believe it! I'm always wrong. How come I have to be right this time?

"You want that paper, young lady?" says the fat man behind the counter. My brain is in a terrible turmoil. What's happening? *How* did it happen? 1944? Somebody— anybody—help! But all I can say to the man is, "No . . . —uh, thank you. That's all right. I just wanted to use the phone."

"Right behind you." He points to a wall phone next to the candy counter. And I think, Grandma, you were never righter. Talk about the wrong time and the wrong place! It's even dumb to call, I tell myself, but so what, I've got nothing to lose. Have I? Probably there'll be no answer anyway. Still, this whole thing is so nutty maybe there's something else I didn't think of, like just suppose it isn't 1944 all over. I mean, maybe it's only here in Queens. That's no crazier than anything else that's happened, is it? Besides, the fat man is looking at me like I'm a loony so I'd better use the phone before he starts asking questions.

I count to 13, which is my lucky number, and start dialing Judson 5-8745 . . . one ring . . . two rings . . . three rings. . . . My God, someone's answering!

"What number are you dialing, please?"

Bummer. It's the operator. I'm so nutty. I dialed wrong. I tell her, "Sorry," hang up and dial again. This time I'm very careful.

"What number are you dialing, please?"

Again. I must really be some kind of jerk, but I swear I dialed it perfectly. "Judson 5-8745," I tell the operator.

"One moment, please."

My luck, it's probably out of order. No wonder no one answered all this time. I should have thought of that. I'll bet they've been going out of their heads worrying about why I didn't call. Oh, boy . . .

"I am sorry, madam. There is no such number."

"You're kidding. It's gotta be. It's my own number. Maybe you didn't hear me right. I said Judson 5- . . ."

"8745."

"Right."

"I am sorry, madam, we show no such number."

"Hey, wait, I forgot to say that's Manhattan, not Queens."

"Madam, our listings cover all five boroughs."

"Well, you gotta be looking it up wrong because that's my own number and we've had it for as long as I can remember, so you see there has to be some mistake. Please look it up again."

"Madam, if you give me your party's name, I will check the number."

"This is silly, I mean, I know the number's right."

"Very well, madam."

"No, wait, please. The name's Martin. Philip Martin."

"One moment, please."

This has got to be the wildest thing. That's absolutely my number. I mean a person doesn't forget the number they've had practically all their lives.

"I'm sorry, madam, we have no listing for Philip Martin."

"You gotta. I mean . . ." Obviously I'm beginning to lose my cool, so I take a deep breath and very calmly ask her to check 81 Central Park West for that name. Of course, no matter how dumb she is, she's got to find our name at that address. Unless . . .

"Madam, we have no 81 Central Park West."

Help!

"Now, look, Operator. You just have to look it up again."

"I'm sorry, madam."

"Will you stop calling me madam. I'm not even fourteen yet."

"Is there another spelling?"

"On my own name? Do you think I'm a moron or something?"

"I'm sorry, madam."

"I told you, I'm not a . . . oh, forget it."

And I crash the phone down hard. Remind me to change my lucky number. Thirteen stinks. For a change my eyes are all watery. You probably think I cry a lot but I can't help it this time. I've got this really lost empty feeling, and worse than that, I feel like there's no hope anymore. I mean, it's all true. This is definitely the forties and I have no home and no family and I'm going to be stuck here forever. That's plenty hard to take.

# Eight

"Hey, is anything wrong?" I didn't even notice Cici come into the store and now she's standing there staring at me. I do a few dumb things like blowing my nose and scratching my eyes so she won't see that I've been crying. I'm sure I don't fool her one bit.

"They're not home." I have to tell her something.

"It's still early, don't worry. You can try again when we get to my house. C'mon, let's go. We're almost there."

And we go outside and start walking up the hill.

"Cici! Hey, Cici!"

About fifty feet behind us two girls about our age are shouting to Cici.

"Hey, wait up!" they call, running up to us.

We stop to wait for them, and Cici tells me that they're friends from her class.

"What's buzzin', cousin?" the taller one says when they reach us. Then they both just stop and stare at me.

Cici takes over the introductions. "This is my friend Victoria and she's staying over at my house, maybe for the weekend." That's the first I've heard of any weekend. My own feeling is that I got to get hold of my mother and get back home. I mean deep, deep down I know this is all goofy and that she's waiting for me someplace. But I don't say anything.

"Victoria, this is Betty," she says, nodding to a skinny girl with short stringy hair that almost looks dirty, "and this is Joyce." Joyce is cute but kind of stuck-up looking.

I'm sort of surprised that Cici's friends are so gross. I'll have to ask her about them later.

In the most outrageous naa-naa voice, Joyce, Miss Snot, who is really too much, tells Cici that she and Betty have been studying practically nonstop since last night.

"I don't know how you're going to do it with those notes you've got," says Betty with such a giggle in her voice that I'd like to push my hand in her dumb face.

Whatever exam they're talking about is really getting to Cici. She starts to squirm and tries to change the subject real fast, but Joyce isn't about to let her.

"You gotta tell Cici to show you her notes," she says to me. "They're the cat's pajamas." And both she and Betty double over in hysterics.

Obviously Cici's notes are horrendous.

"Wish I could lend you mine," Joyce says, gloating so much I may throw up, "but I'll be using them all weekend. Sorry."

"Yeah, well, that's okay. I've got a lot of it in my head already and besides . . . uh . . ." Cici is sort of scrambling around for some way to recover. She finds it. "Victoria's going to help me."

No way. Unless she's only getting a D and wants an F. Of course, I don't say any of that. I just stand there trying to look very scientific.

"She's a straight-A science student . . ."

There she goes. Miss Overkill.

". . . in fact, she's so far ahead that she's already finished all her biology and chemistry and she's started first-year trigonometry."

"Trigonometry?" Joyce announces, real smart-ass. "Funny, I always thought that was math."

"You mean you really thought astral trig was math?" I say brilliantly. "How amusing." There's this magnificent silence while we all watch Joyce's jaw drop down to her knees. Cici is so pleased with me I'm afraid she may break into applause and spoil the whole scene. I feel sensational.

"Hey, look, we're really late," Cici says. "We gotta get home. See you tonight at the party."

"See you later," I say.

You should see their faces at the thought of an extra girl at their precious party.

"Is she coming?" Betty asks Cici, giving her eyes that "Oh, God" roll.

Cici's not about to listen to any more jazz from these two, so she tells them straight out, "If you don't like it, lump it." And she gives me a little shove and we start running up the hill.

At the top of the hill we turn into a quiet street with big old oak trees. On one side are old wooden frame houses, and on the other, the uphill side, are huge fortress-like brick homes each set about fifty feet up from the sidewalk. They're all big and dark and sort of loom over the street. Sounds scary but it isn't. In fact, they're kind of silly-looking because the structures are so gigantic and the property is so tiny that the houses practically have to hold their breath to fit on the land.

Cici's head is down as we walk along the block, and I think she's forgotten all about me. I feel a little uncomfortable because, you know, I'm very dependent on her.

"Hey!" she says, and suddenly the kookiness is back in her face and I know what she's been doing. She's been cooking up a new plan. "Come here," she says, and she pulls me into one of the open garages. "Want one?" she says, coming up with a short unfiltered cigarette from some side pocket of her bag. It's a little crushed but otherwise perfectly smokable. There's no point in ruining her surprise by telling her that I hate unfiltered cigarettes. They make me even more nauseous than filtered ones, which do a pretty good job on my stomach.

She lights the cigarette and takes a puff and hands it to me.

"Want a drag?" she says.

Naturally I can't refuse. I take the tiniest puff possible, hold it in my mouth for a couple of seconds, and then slowly let it kind of leak out between my teeth. There's got to be a better way. I hand it back to Cici, who takes another drag.

"Do you inhale?" she asks me, trying to be real cool as the smoke pours out of her nose and winds its way right into her eyes. "Ohh . . . that stings."

"That happens to me all the time," I tell her, but she's too busy jumping around and rubbing her eyes. "And it's worse when I inhale. I get so dizzy I think I'm going to fall over."

"Me too. Sometimes after dinner I sneak up to the bathroom for a butt and I get so woozy that the floor tiles start rolling up and down."

"I'm probably not going to be a smoker. It's really bad for you."

"Yeah? Where'd you hear that?"

Cici has this way of kidding with a deadpan face. At first I didn't know when she was joking, but now I think I can tell.

"Except grass." I keep a straight face too. "Now that's really good for you."

"Real healthy," she says, "if you're a cow."

"I mean pot, dope."

"Hey!" Suddenly she looks insulted. Oh, boy, we're on different wavelengths. She probably never heard of pot or . . . wow! she must think I'm calling her a dope. No way to explain so I change the subject fast.

"I don't think those two creeps, Betty and what's-her-face, Joyce, were too happy about me going to the party tonight."

"TS. If they don't like it, they can lump it."

"Yeah, TS." I'm beginning to sound 1940. "Those two really turn me off. Did you see what a charge they were getting out of bugging you about that science test? Gross."

"Ugh! Don't even mention it. Old Horseface Davis—she's my teacher—said that if I don't get a seventy-five on it, she's going to flunk me and then I won't graduate. Can you just see me left back? Doing 8 B again? I'd die first."

"Unreal!"

"I wish Horseface was. She's such a rat fink and she hates me, which is really unfair because I've been trying very hard lately. I even did a project for extra credit—some dumb thing with an egg and a glass jar. What a flop! How was I supposed to know the egg had to be hard-boiled? You should have seen her face when she tried to do the experiment."

It must have been horrendous because just the memory of it makes Cici break up.

"And then to top things off, I get hysterical. I knew I was in real trouble and it wasn't funny, but sometimes I get this thing where I can't stop laughing."

"Yeah. I know exactly what you mean." It's always such a relief to find someone as nutty as you are.

"That's when she exploded and gave me the ultimatum about getting a seventy-five on the final. That stinks because except for her classes, all my other marks are great. Oh, well, maybe sewing is a little problem.''

"You mean that thing in your bag?"

"Yeah, my graduation dress."

I don't believe it. I mean, I'm freaking out at the thought of someone actually wearing that rag. And for graduation no less. Naturally I don't say anything, but I guess she sees it in my face because she shrugs and says, "I know, I hate sewing even worse than science."

I would say that's pretty obvious, except I don't. All I say is, "I wish I could help you, but science is a bummer for me, too. The minute someone mentions anything even vaguely scientific, I turn right off."

"Me too. Only I turn so far off that I even forget to take notes. Like now, I'm really up the creek because I'm missing half the notes and the other half is so crummy that I can hardly read them."

"Can't you borrow somebody else's notes?"

"No can do. Everybody needs their own notes. Oh, well, you can't go crazy."

That's what my mother always says, "You can't go crazy," but I think I would if I wasn't going to graduate. "What are you going to do?"

"I'll figure something out, I guess."

Something's fishy. I mean, she's much too cool. I'm really curious, so I level with her. "How come you don't seem so worried?" One look at her face and I can tell I'm right. She's got something up her sleeve.

"Yeah, well''—she looks at me real hard, like she's deciding something—"I guess I'm not."

"How come?" I'm not letting go because now I'm really curious.

"You won't say anything?"

"Are you kidding?"

"Well, this is really secret stuff. I'm finished if even a word gets out."

"I swear to God and hope to die I won't breathe a word of it."

"I'm getting the test," she whispers.

"What do you mean?"

"This kid Ted's giving me the test." She's looking over her shoulder like she expects the CIA any second. Then she says, even softer, "His mom's my teacher."

"Far out! Wow! I wouldn't have the guts for something like that. Aren't you scared you'll get caught?"

"Plenty scared. Don't even remind me. I start to sweat just thinking about it. Boy, I'd die if anyone ever found out. Of course I'd probably be expelled instantly, but what's even worse, my parents would be absolutely crushed. I know I'm not perfect but I've never done anything like *this* before. It's almost like being a criminal, but I can't help it, I'm trapped. I gotta graduate."

"What if he tells someone—like brags? You know how boys are."

"Yeah, I know, but Ted's no kid, he's almost eighteen, and besides he'd be in as much hot water as me. After all, he's doing the stealing, right?"

"I guess so, but it's taking a big chance anyhow."

"You don't know how big. I gotta trust Ted and, boy, is he a crud. For a teacher's kid he's almost a JD. I mean it. He practically dropped out of high school last year, and he hangs around with a real tough crowd. And you want to hear the payoff?"

"Yeah."

"He likes me. Ugh!"

"Is that how come he's doing this for you?"

"Are you kidding? I'm paying him a mint. That's how

come. I didn't even ask him to do it. He must have heard about it from some of the kids because one time about a week ago we were all in Pop Stiller's malt shop and he pulls me aside and says, 'I'll get it for you.' I didn't even know what he was talking about at first so I said something like, 'Yeah, I'll bet you will,' and started to walk away, but then he followed me and whispered that he'd get the science test for me and I nearly fainted.''

Cici took another drag on the cigarette and coughed three or four times. She handed it to me. This time I inhaled, and *I* nearly fainted. She didn't notice.

''At first I thought he was pulling my leg, but then when I saw he was serious I said forget it—I'm not going to get involved in anything like that—and I just walked away. Then when I got home I started thinking about not graduating. How would I ever face my family or my friends again? And then I thought about when I was in 6 B and Harold Klinger got left back.''

''They don't do that anymore,'' I tell Cici.

''Do what?''

''Leave you back.'' Kick you out, yeah, but nothing primitive like leaving you back.

''Sure they do,'' she says impatiently. ''I just told you they left Harold Klinger back.'' She gives me an odd look but continues on about poor Harold.

''He didn't find out until the last day before summer vacation when we all got our report cards. You know how that's always the best day of the whole term with everyone kidding around, talking and comparing cards? Except Harold. He just sat in his seat, and his face was getting redder and redder, even his ears, and then suddenly he burst into tears—the real sobbing kind where you can't catch your breath. It was horrible. Then Mr. Bernard, who was a real rat, said to him, no sympathy, nothing, just, 'Harold, I think you'd better step out into the hall until you can control yourself.' Harold was crying so hard he could barely find the door.''

The cigarette was burning down. I handed it back to Cici. "He must have been real dumb," I say.

"Yeah, but even so, I felt real sorry for him. Everybody did. It was awful what getting left back did to him. He used to be the class joker and very popular, but he didn't make any friends in his new class, and when you'd meet him in the halls, he was so embarrassed he could barely look at you. I finally stopped saying anything to him because it made him so uncomfortable. And that was only being left back in 6 B. When it happens in 8 B and you don't graduate and all your friends go on to high school and you gotta come back to grammar school, it's the worst thing in the whole world. That's when I made up my mind. No matter what, it's not going to happen to me, even if I have to cheat. . . . I don't care. I gotta graduate."

Poor Cici. She's probably found the most sympathetic ear in the whole country. But as bad as my own school problems are, at least I'm not involved in any stealing. Now I feel sort of squirmy for her, so I ask her if maybe there isn't another way out. Like suppose she talked to the teacher. Or maybe took a make-up test.

"With old Horseface?" Cici is shaking her head like I'm nuts. "Not even if I broke down and cried. Her greatest joy in life is the sight of tears. It's hopeless. There's no other way. If I don't get that test, I'm going to fail for sure."

"What if I helped you? Suppose we really crammed all night and all day tomorrow?"

"With my notes I could cram for about seven minutes."

"Hey, I got it. Let's Xerox somebody's. It only takes a minute."

"Huh? What's a Xerox?"

Oh, wow! That was dumb. They probably didn't even invent the Xerox machine yet. I have to make up something quick because it sounds like a way out, so she's really curious.

"It's a city word for putting the snatch on something." I could go on and tell how it's named after this famous robber, Jason Xerox, but I can tell she's not interested. So instead I ask her, "What about telling your parents and asking them if they can do something with the teacher?"

"No good. You don't know my parents, especially my mother. I'd never hear the end of it . . . and besides it wouldn't work. Horseface hates parents worse than kids. There's just no other way, Victoria. I know, because all I've been doing for the last five days is thinking about this thing and I've got no choice. I gotta get that exam and that's all there is to it."

I guess there's no point in telling her what bad vibes I get from just thinking about the plan. She's really trapped. She has to take the gamble, but I'm sort of scared for her.

We're so busy with our conversation that the cigarette burns out before either of us has a chance to really smoke it. Super. I hated it anyway. I only do it for effect. I mean, I think I look very mature smoking.

"Let's go," Cici says, picking up her pocketbook. "I live just a few houses down."

We walk down the street about four houses. At the fifth house Cici stops.

"Up here's where I live."

Up here turns out to be a huge square stack of dark red bricks in the shape of a house—you know, the kind you draw when you're about five years old. Two stories high, door in the center, double windows upstairs and down, and smack in the middle of the roof, the chimney. It's not very beautiful but it sure looks solid. You could huff and puff forever and it'd still be there.

"Hey, look, Victoria . . . uh . . ."

I can see Cici's really freaked out, I mean about telling me her secret. Now she's scared I'll let it slip. Of course I assure her it's absolutely safe with me. Cross my heart and hope to die.

"I'm sorry, Victoria, but you're the only other person who knows and—well, it occurred to me that I really don't know you all that well and . . . oh forget it, that was jerky. I knew the minute I met you that you were going to be my friend . . . my special friend . . . and that I could trust you with anything."

That's the way I feel about Cici too, but I'm not ready to tell her my secret yet. Not until I'm absolutely certain that I'm not nuts.

"Let's go," she says, and starts up the steep flight of brick steps.

"Hey, wait." I stop midflight. "I forgot to ask you about your family."

"Shoot."

"Well, do you have any sisters or brothers?"

"First there's my brother, the meanest, most despicable, lowest form of creepy crud tease in the Western Hemisphere. Then there's my mother. I told you a little about her. She's in charge of the house and the kids—that's me and the creep. She's a regular mother type—you know, tells you when to eat, what to eat, where to go, when to come home, what to wear, and when to breathe. Other than that, you're completely on your own. As for my dad, he's the policy-maker, the great white father. Actually I love my parents. Until lately anyway. Now all we do is fight. They just don't realize that I'm not a baby anymore. I'm fourteen and my mother's got to stop hanging over me like I'm a two-year-old.''

"Stop. I know just what you mean. My mother does the same exact thing and it really grosses me out.''

"I figure she's probably just going through a stage, but I don't know if I can wait for her to outgrow it.''

Cici opens the door. Standing in the center hall, I can see a large living room on one side and the dining room on the other. In front of me is a flight of stairs leading to the second floor. There's a lot of yellows and golds and oranges, and everything looks solid like the house, neat and clean and homey. Cici goes up a couple of steps and calls out. "Mommy! Ma! I'm home and I've got a friend with me.''

"I'll be right down.''

# Nine

My God! That voice slams into my stomach like a two-by-four. I can't catch my breath. Luckily, Cici is facing the steps and doesn't see me. It's that voice. Oh, God! You won't believe this, but I know it! I'd know it anywhere, any time. It's so unreal . . . oh, let it be a dream. I squeeze my eyes as hard as I can, then open them crazy wide, pinch my hand, and will my mind to wake up. But nothing happens. You know that sort of liquid quality you feel in a dream where everything kind of flows and changes easily? Well, there's nothing flowing or fuzzy or hazy or anything less than dead real here, in this hall, in this house, at this minute.

And there's another thing. This minute. This damn very minute is happening right now thirty years ago. It's the creepiest thing that's ever happened to me, and I'm really shook up because now I know that it's not a dream and soon that woman is going to come down those stairs and I don't know whether to scream or run away or what. I've never been so scared in all my life and nothing's happening. I mean, I'm not crying or running or anything. Only sweating and standing here like an idiot, waiting.

"Come on. I'll make you a malted." Cici's voice startles me. I forgot she was even there. Now I stare at her. Who is she anyway?

"Don't you like malteds?" I guess I didn't answer her. I'm busy trying to work up enough spit for a swallow to get my tongue off the roof of my mouth and say something. No sound comes out. All I can manage to do is nod my head and follow her through the dining room into an enormous kitchen and stand there like some kind of jerk while she starts making a malted in a real malted machine like the kind they have in drugstores.

"Chocolate ice cream all right?" she asks. This time my head bobs up and down like a mechanical toy and she looks at me kind of funny. I stop the stupid head-nodding, but I still can't speak because if I open my mouth even a crack I know I'm going to burst out crying. I just stand here trying to think of a million other things, but it's no use. Big blobs of tears are crowding my eyes, but luckily Cici doesn't look up from the malteds.

"Hey, listen," she says. "If my mother asks where we've been all day, just say the movies. Forget about all the rest, including the matron and Mr. Hot Pants, okay?"

Before I can answer (which I couldn't do anyway) that voice from upstairs calls out, "Hello, hello."

"Here, Mommy, in the kitchen."

There's a sound of footsteps coming down the stairs. At first they're far away at the top and they sound soft, but they get harder and sharper as they clip-clap their way down. I hold my breath to hear better. Now they're at the bottom and the sound of them pounds in my head. She's coming. I panic. And now there's something else reaching for me, something worse, another thought, but I push it away, too frightened to let it in.

"Cici . . . the bathroom. Where's the bathroom? Quick, I don't feel so good."

"Right there." She points to a door right off the kitchen.
I rush for it and slam the door behind me just as the
footsteps come through the dining room and into the kitchen.

The bathroom is tiny with barely enough room for the
toilet, a small sink, and me. The rest of the space looks
like it's being devoured by the wallpaper, a gaudy jungle
of the biggest orange and yellow mums I've ever seen.
There's a tacky little gold-framed mirror straight ahead of
me and I stare hard into it. Maybe it'll be like an Alice-
through-the-looking-glass thing and if I concentrate hard
enough I'll be able to walk right into the mirror and come
out the other side, in the seventies in my own house.
That's really not so far out when you consider how weird
everything else has been. But no luck. Nothing happens,
except the dumb face looking back at me is getting blotch-
ier and sweatier and more scared-looking.

I can hear the voices in the kitchen but I can't make out
what they're saying. I try not to imagine. I flush the toilet
so they don't get too suspicious. I need time to think. I
have to get out of here somehow. But the only possible
way is through the porthole-size window over the sink.
I'm on the first floor so there's no real drop, but I don't
know if I can squeeze through. Maybe if I can open it all
the way. . . . Forget it. There are two large screws on both
sides of the frame that keep it from opening any more than
four inches.

"Hey, Victoria." It's Cici's voice. "Are you okay?" I
try to answer but the most I can do is shake my head
emphatically, which of course she can't hear. A couple of
seconds go by and she calls my name again.

"Victoria? Coming out?"

I have no choice. I can't stay here forever. I splash
some cold water on my face, but I'm still pretty splotchy-

looking. I pull up my socks, comb my hair, tighten my belt, smear on some lipgloss, blow my nose, and wipe out the sink where a couple of hairs have fallen. By now my socks have fallen again.

"Victoria?" Oh my God. It's that voice again. "Are you sick, dear?"

I take a very deep breath and start to unlock the door and squeak it open inch by inch. This approach is excruciating, like going into an icy pool bit by bit. The only way to do it is to throw the door open all at once. One. Two. Three. And I do it. Nothing. The door is wide open but there's no one there. Maybe they vanished. Maybe it's all over. Or maybe they're just standing on the other side of the kitchen where I can't see them. I walk the four short steps into the kitchen and . . . there they are.

She's beautiful. Her hair is dark brown with soft shiny curls that almost touch her shoulders. Her cheeks look sort of flushed, they're so pink. She's wearing a silky striped blouse that matches the orangy red of her lipstick. She smiles at me, and her gray eyes sort of squint like they always do when she doesn't wear her glasses. She comes toward me, friendly, welcoming, a fragrant aroma of Arpège, and whoosh—that icy wind shoots through my stomach. I can't stop myself. I back away. In all my life, since as far back as I can remember, this is the first time I have ever been afraid of my own grandmother.

That's who she is. Sure, she's younger and slimmer and all that. But there's no question. I know for absolutely certain that she's my grandma. And that has to mean—no! I won't let the thought come any closer. It can't be!

"How nice to meet you, Victoria."

My very own grandmother says that like it's the first time she ever laid eyes on me in her life. And of course it is! I'm positively freaked out. If she comes any closer I might scream or, more likely, throw myself into her arms and just hang there for dear life. She takes a step nearer, but I don't budge. I just stay in one spot, a big blob glued to the floor.

Oh, Grandma, can't you see? It's me, Victoria. Why don't you know me, your own granddaughter? Don't you love me? (Dumb. How can she love me when she doesn't even know me?)

"Don't worry dear, we'll be able to get in touch with your parents. In the meantime just make yourself comfortable and try not to worry too much." She says the whole thing in a kind but formal voice. It's hopeless. She hasn't got the vaguest idea who I am. Then she turns to Cici and says, "I know Felicia is delighted to have you stay with us in the meantime."

Felicia! Not Cici. Felicia! I let the thought in now because there's no way to fight it. I turn and stare at Cici.

"Victoria? Is something wrong?" One of their voices comes through to me and I think I shake my head.

Felicia! Cici! My own mother! Holy cow, am I dumb. It had to be. Fantastic! I told you she looked familiar. I mean, she didn't really, but there were things about her that reminded me of someone. Not so much the features, but more like the expressions, the way she talked—I don't know what, something, maybe the look in her eyes. I just knew I knew her all along, only I thought she was a friend of somebody's or some girl I met someplace. That's what threw me. I thought she was a kid like me.

But she's not. She's a woman. Felicia, Cici, whatever she wants to call herself, there's one thing for sure, this crazy nutty kid who isn't afraid to zonk a pervert in the shin, turn Woolworth's upside down, sneak cigarettes in a garage, and probably do a million other kooky things and maybe even some awful things like buying a science test, isn't my friend at all.

She's my *mother*!

# *Ten*

By now you probably figure I've flipped my lid. Well, so do I, but it doesn't change things. Right this minute I'm looking straight at my mother, only she's fourteen years old. I mean it's fantastic that I'm looking into the very same yellow-brown eyes that I've looked into thousands of times before. I don't know how come I didn't recognize that special look they have. I think I even see it now. Her hair throws me a little. My mother's is blonder and curlier now, but I guess a little bleach and some curlers handle that pretty easily. And her chin. It sticks out just like my mother's. Hey, jerk, it isn't *just like*—it *is* my mother's chin.

Well, so far so good. I mean they're just standing there. Nobody's attacking me so maybe it's not going to be so bad. In fact I think I feel a little better now. Not so scared. After all, it is my mother and grandmother, and even if they don't know who I am, still, they're not exactly killer monsters. Actually they're terrific people. All my friends think they're super. Whenever I go to visit my grandmother's country club, everybody is always telling me how sensational she is. And my mother? I told you before I'm the only one who doesn't like her. Except now. Now she turns out to be my best friend. So why am I still shaking?

"Aaah!" Cici says, making a grab for the overflowing

malted machine. I jump a foot straight into the air. I guess I'm still a little scared.

"How many times do I have to tell you not to fill it so high," my grandmother says, sounding more like my mother than my grandmother. "Here." She hands Cici the sponge. "Before it drips on the floor."

Cici wipes the counter and fills two glasses with mostly foam and hands one to me. I figure I gotta make myself talk or they're going to think I'm some kind of a moron.

"Thank you," I say. It isn't much but it's all I can manage now in my condition. I really hope my grandmother, or Mrs. Lyons (I guess that's what I'll have to call her now), just thinks I'm shy, not unfriendly. I know she's not going to love me in a day, but I do want her to like me.

"Victoria, would you like to try your house again?" She sounds like she likes me okay.

"Yes, please," I say, squinching my mouth in smile formation, I hope.

"Felicia, let Victoria use the hall phone."

We finish our malteds.

"After you've called, Felicia will introduce you to her brother."

An "ugh" sound plus an "ugh" look is Cici's answer.

"I don't like that, Felicia." That's exactly what my mother says to me when I do something like that about Nina. But what's really incredible is how my mother is about her brother now. I'm talking about the 1970s. I told you how close they are, practically like twins. Uncle Steve can do no wrong. And she's always saying how she would do anything for him and he would do anything for her. In fact, she's always using him as an example of how siblings are supposed to act toward each other. Wow! What baloney. Wait till I tell her. . . . What am I talking about? Who am I going to tell? Cici? My fourteen-year-old mother? Sure,

I'll just tell her everything. I'll just go right up to her and say, "Hey, Cici, you may not believe this but . . . you're my mother."

"Of course, dear," she'll say. "Now, if you'll just step over here these nice men with the nets want to have a word with you."

We go into the hall and Cici shows me the telephone.

"Come upstairs to my room when you're finished." And Cici heads up the steps.

I haven't even got the nerve to dial my own number, so I just make up any old number and call it. Lucky for me, there's no answer.

"Victoria!" Cici pokes her head out from the top of the steps. "Any luck?"

"Nope. Still not home."

"They'll probably be home by tonight," she says, coming down the stairs. "You know you can stay here as long as you want."

How's fifty years for starters?

"Anyway," she says, "I was sort of hoping you could stay over for the weekend. I really want you to go to that party tonight."

"Me too." I guess I'm a lousy actress because she looks at me funny.

"Victoria, I think something else is bothering you. Ever since we got home you've been acting sort of—I don't know—scared. Look, you're my good friend, so I'm not going to BS you. You're going to think I'm crazy but . . . uh . . . well, are you afraid of my mother?"

"Afraid of your mother?" I guess I didn't fool her, but I deny it like crazy. "Of course not. I think your mother's terrific, really sensational." This time I really sound convincing, and why shouldn't I? She's my own grandmother and

I really do think she's super. "I just felt kind of worried about barging in like this. You know, not invited and all."

"Forget it. She doesn't mind at all. Wow, that's a load off my mind. I really was worried that you hated it here and especially my mother. I know I have some complaints about her, but, gee, she isn't exactly a killer monster."

Where have I heard that before?

I smile and she seems satisfied and we go up the stairs. At the top to the left is what must be my grandparents' room. I follow Cici down a long hall past a small bedroom and then to Cici's room. It doesn't look like her at all. It's really large and elegantly decorated with heavy silk drapes right down to the floor, a delicate crystal chandelier, and, my God, there's my dresser! It's the one from my room at home, the one I've had since as far back as I can remember. The only difference is that on this one the white marble top is in perfect condition. Mine got cracked when we tried to move it a couple of years ago. I've always known it belonged to my mother when she was a kid, but it's so weird to actually see it here in her room. I can't believe my clothes aren't in the drawers.

The room is spotless. I mean absolutely perfect, couldn't be neater. What a disappointment. Well, nobody's perfect. Actually I should have suspected because my mother's always nagging me to clean my room.

"Here's some space for you to dump your stuff," Cici says, opening the middle drawer of the dresser. The entire inside of the drawer is a mass of rolled-up lumps of clothes jammed together. Gross! I love it. She digs her hand in one corner and shoves them over to make room for my things, only she can't shove much because it's so over-loaded already, and the only way I can possibly get my clothes in is to roll them up and stuff them in. Cici holds her things back while I squeeze mine in and then together we slide the drawer shut quickly, tucking in the hangouts. No problem. I've been doing it for years.

"Nice going," she says, and I'm beginning to feel really comfortable, what with my own dresser and all. The all is the mirror. I didn't notice before but that's my mirror too.

"I'd better hide these butts in the secret drawer," Cici says, and starts to scramble through her pocketbook while I open the "secret drawer" for her. It's a great hiding place. It's impossible to tell by looking at the dresser that there's a fourth drawer at the bottom because it has no handles and it's disguised as a panel. In fact, you have to slide your fingers underneath to pull it open. Nobody ever knows. . . . So how come I know? Ooh, that was dumb.

"You're the first person who ever knew about that drawer without my showing them," Cici says, shaking her head in amazement. "How did you know it was there?"

No sweat. I tell her the absolute truth. "I have the exact same dresser."

"No kidding."

"Swear to God. It's identical, even has the same round mirror." It feels fantastic to be actually telling the complete truth about something. All this secret-keeping can really make you uptight. "Mine even has that fancy trim on the edge of the mirror."

"No fooling?"

"Right. And those identical tiny little flower things too."

"I'm really surprised . . ."

"It's absolutely incredible, but it's got to be the same exact set . . ."

". . . because it's not a set. We bought the mirror separately."

"Except that my mirror is a lot rounder than yours and

smaller. In fact it's only half the size and the flowers are so tiny you can barely make them out. Actually they look more like butterflies with extra wings.'' I'm wishing somebody would stuff an old sock in my mouth or the house would catch fire or something so I could stop. No way. ''Truthfully it's more like a picture than a mirror. I suppose that's why we keep it in the living room.''

One of the best things about Cici is that she doesn't get thrown easily. She sees she's dealing with a raving lunatic whose face is probably getting redder and hotter by the second and whose mouth won't stop, so with spectacular compassion and great cool, she just cuts in and changes the subject.

''I gotta get out of these things or they're going to be all cruddy for tonight.'' And with that she unbuttons her skirt, casually lets it slide to the floor, and steps out of it. The blouse she lets fall in another heap a couple of feet away. Too much. Would you believe my mother, who is forever bugging me to clean my room, is a worse pig than I am? At least I aim for the chair. Of course sometimes the chair gets pretty loaded and a few things might slip to the floor, but that's different.

Cici pulls a pair of short shorts and a T-shirt out of the top drawer (we even keep our shirts in the same drawer) and starts to put them on. You wouldn't believe the shorts. They're made of some kind of real sleazy white material with horrendous puckery gathers at the waist and pleats in front and back. Are they gross. I can see her eyeing my jeans.

''If you want to change, I've got a million pairs of shorts, or how about a pair of pedal pushers?''

Ugh . . . I wouldn't be caught dead in those grungy shorts. I don't even know what pedal pushers are, but they sound too cute for words so I pass them up too. Another nice thing about my mother as a kid unlike my mother as a mother is that she doesn't push. No nagging. Whatever I want is okay with her. How did she change so drastically?

Suddenly the door is pushed open by a raunchy-looking guy of about sixteen.

"Knock, you jerk." My mother greets what has to be my Uncle Steve, the brother she would do anything in the world for.

"Drop dead, fink," is his loving answer. "Where's my new Submariner?"

"I haven't got the vaguest," she sneers.

"Liar." The natural answer. I'm happy to say this is the first time I'm really beginning to feel at home.

"I am not. You put one smelly foot over that threshold and I'm telling," says my mother.

"Where's my comic?"

"I don't know, and if you don't like it you can lump it."

"It may be true for all we know," he starts to sing a really annoying song, "but it sounds like bull to me . . ."

"Shut up and get out!"

". . . so take that crap to another sap and stop . . ."

"I'm telling . . ."

". . . bullshitting me."

"Maa!" she screams.

We all just stand there looking at each other. As soon as there's a silence any place I always feel like I have to fill it, so I look at Uncle Steve and say, "Hi, I'm Victoria." In the middle of the whole fight I got to be Miss Manners. Naturally he looks at me like I'm some kind of a roach and grunts, "Yeah," and loses interest. I hate him already. I can't believe he's so gross.

"Drop dead," he says to Cici, and starts to walk away.

How dare he talk to my mother like that! I'll never forgive him.

"Ma!" she screams, and races out of the room and down the hall, shouting for my grandmother in my sister Nina's best "I'm-being-murdered" voice.

My ex-favorite uncle takes off pretty quick, and by the time my grandmother gets upstairs he's safely back in his room with the door shut.

"How many times do I have to tell you to stay out of your sister's room?" my grandmother says, opening Uncle Steve's door. And to my mother: "I can't leave you two alone for two minutes without trouble. Aren't you embarrassed to have your friend see you behaving like a two-year-old?"

If she wasn't embarrassed before, she certainly is now. So am I. At least I can see where my mother learned her mother phrases. But, funny thing, my grandmother seems to have forgotten them. I never hear her talk like that now. I just had a horrendous thought. Maybe mother-talk is something you use for a while, then pass on to your daughter, and one day I'll be sounding like that. No way! I swear it.

Now my grandmother studies me closely, squinting even though she has her glasses on this time, and I get the strong feeling maybe she's going to recognize me. Of course that's dumb—how could she? I haven't even been born yet. Instead, she shakes her head and smiles and says, "You know, you two look enough alike to be sisters."

Both of us look in my big mirror above the dresser. Funny, people are always saying I look like my mother but I could never see it. Now I can. I mean, we really do look alike, almost the same color hair, and we both have oval-shaped faces. I don't know but for the first time I can really see the resemblance. And it's eerie.

"Felicia," my grandmother says, zeroing in on the pile of clothes on the floor, "don't leave this room without putting your clothes away."

There's only one sentence in the world that can follow those instructions, and it begins, "How many times do I have to tell you . . ."

"How many times do I have to tell you to hang up your clothes when you take them off?" Of course that's my grandmother talking. What did I tell you?

"I said I will," my mother whines.

"Don't let me walk in here and see them on the floor again." I think they're reading from a script.

My grandmother stands in the doorway, hands on her hips, waiting. With a hopeless shrug my mother bends down and starts to gather up her clothes. Satisfied, my grandmother turns to leave. "I have a Red Cross meeting. I should be home in a couple of hours. If Daddy calls tell him I'll meet him at the ration board."

The minute my grandmother goes out of the door, Cici rolls her eyes and whispers, "Isn't she the cat's pajamas? Is your mother as bad as mine? I mean, is she always nagging you about how your room should be and things like that?"

Far out! Now my mother is asking me to tell her all the horrendous things about herself. I ask you, does that blow your mind or doesn't it?

"Are you kidding?" I'm not about to pass this one up. "Nobody in the whole world"—if she only knew!—"can bug you like my mother. All I have to do is leave one little soda can under my bed and she practically goes berserk. It's her big thing. She's a neatness freak. Of course she's also a homework freak and an on-time freak and a don't-borrow-anybody's-clothes freak and a don't-fight-with-your-sister freak, and that's only the beginning. Honestly, I swear I'm never going to be that way with my kid. How about you?''

"Me? Fat chance. I told you, I plan on being the most terrific mother that ever was.''

"How are you going to do that?''

"Easy. Like with her room. It's hers and she can keep it anyway she wants.''

"You mean that?''

"You bet. Not only that, I'm never going to just barge in without knocking. The way I feel, a person's room is her own private property and that's that.''

"Even if it's filled with dirty laundry and old grungy leftover food?''

"Well,'' Cici says with a tiny hesitation I'm not too crazy about, "maybe then I'd ask her to empty it once a week or something like that.''

"What if she forgets?''

"Then I'd remind her.''

"Suppose she keeps forgetting.''

"Then I'd keep reminding her.''

"Probably she'd say you were nagging.''

When I say that she really breaks up. In fact we both burst out laughing.

"You know what?'' she says, still laughing, "she'd probably be right. I can just hear me.'' And then she turns to me like I was her kid and, hand on hip, finger shaking, and sounding for absolute real, says, "Victoria, this room is a pigsty. How many times do I have to remind you to hang up your clothes, and take that empty Coke bottle out of here this instant!''

"Help! Stop! You sound just like my mother.''

"God forbid!'' And we both get hysterical again. Except maybe it's not so funny.

"What about other things?'' I figure I'm never going to

get this opportunity again so I charge ahead. "I mean like curfews and school work and being on time, and what if she accidentally on purpose pushes her pain-in-the-ass sister down in the railroad station . . . what about those things?"

Now she gets kind of serious. "The way I figure, I'm going to take very good care of my child when she's little, but when she gets about our age she can run things for herself so I'm not going to interfere too much. Unless, of course, she needs me."

"My grandmother says that you change your mind about a lot of things when you grow up and have to be responsible for someone else. Especially if that someone is your own child."

"Maybe some people change, but not me. I mean it, I know exactly what kind of mother I'm going to be and I don't see how responsibility is going to make that much difference. Do you?"

"I didn't used to, but now . . . I don't know."

"Oh, well, lucky we don't have to worry about it now. We got tons of time before we're mothers, and while we're waiting . . ." The kooky look is back in her eyes. "Wanna see something neat?" She takes out some black-and-white speckled notebooks and a skinny blue pamphlet. "I'll show you the slam books after. First look at this," and she puts the schoolbooks aside and hands me the pamphlet.

I have no idea what a "slam book" is, and the little blue book she gives me looks like just a bunch of dumb cartoons stapled together. The title on the front is "Wally and the King." I flip through and it turns out to be a comic book about a girl named Wally and a guy with a crown on his head and nothing else. From page two on they're having sex. Big deal!

"What d'ya think?" Cici is really anxious for my reaction so I make it big.

"Wow! That's wild," I say, but I don't really think it. Compared to *The Joy of Sex* or a lot of other stuff you can buy in any bookstore, this is a joke. I mean, it's for five-year-olds, but I guess way back in the forties this was real far out. The only thing I can think of is, "Why do they call the girl Wally?"

"Didn't you ever hear of Wallis Simpson and King Edward?"

Now I'm the dumb one so I just shake my head and say, "I guess not."

"He was the King of England who gave up his throne to marry an American divorcee. You know, the Duke and Duchess of Windsor."

"Oh, yeah, I've heard of them." I really did but I never knew anything about them. "But I just didn't recognize them without their clothes." I try to make a joke so I don't look so jerky.

"My brother Steve has a deck of French cards in a little metal box but he keeps it locked up. I've combed his room from top to bottom a million times when he wasn't around but I still can't find the key."

Things really have changed a lot since my mother was fourteen. All I have to do now is look on the bookshelves in my own house and I can find all the books on sex I want, and they're a lot more explicit than this silly cartoon book.

"And I have something else. Well, I don't have it but Steve does and I've seen it."

Sounds interesting so I ask, "What is it?"

"Did you ever hear of Henry Miller's *Tropic of Cancer*?"

"Sure."

"Well, I know where there's a copy."

Me too. Down the corner at Bookmasters. But of course, I don't say that because it's such a big deal to Cici, so I pretend I'm really freaked out, and that's not easy because I think I'm going to get hysterical in one minute. I mean this is really too much.

"Far out. Let's get it."

"Later, when he goes out. Then we'll look for that key too."

"Cool! Are the slam books porno stuff too?"

Cici laughs and grabs one of the books and shoves it in my hands. "I can't understand how you never heard of slam books. Things must really be different in the city. Here, look through it." And she starts to show me the pages. "See, every page has a heading like cutest, best dresser, funniest, stuff like that. What you do is pass the book around the class and everyone writes in the name of the person they nominate for that category."

"Then what?"

"Then nothing. That's it. It's just fun to see who gets the most votes for anything. Especially the bad things, like who goes the furthest, the fastest, the worst rep—you know, all the awful things."

"Boy, I'd hate to be Janet Foley. She's got her name on all the gross pages. She must be pretty funky."

"You should see her—boobs out to here."

"Felicia! Felicia!" A girl's voice from someplace outside the house is calling my mother.

"That's Carolanne, the kid from next door," she says, sticking her head way out of the window. "Yeah?"

"I got the carriage. Wanna go now?" Carolanne whoever shouts up.

"I promised her I'd go collecting this afternoon," my mother says to me.

"Collecting?"

"You know, silver."

I don't know silver, but I hate to look too dumb so I say, "Yeah, sure."

"It'll only take an hour or so if we go now."

"I'm ready." No big deal missing the rest of that porno jazz.

## *Eleven*

We both shoot downstairs and you wouldn't believe what's waiting outside for us. There's this dumpy little twelve-year-old pudge who's got to be Carolanne pushing a million-year-old doll carriage stuffed full of rolled-up balls of silver paper. I'm smart enough to figure she's either a retardate or a loony so I keep my mouth shut.

"Hubba, hubba," my mother says, and she really looks impressed.

By now she's up to her elbows digging in the mound of silver balls. "You really found the mother lode." Then she turns to me. "Terrif, huh?"

I search her face to see if she's putting me on, but no, she's serious. I figure it's probably safest to play it by ear for now. "Hubba, hubba," I say, just because I can't resist it.

We store the silver Carolanne collected in the garage and start off down the street, pushing this raunchy old carriage. We stop at every house on the block and the people are beautiful. They open the doors right away (mostly they aren't even locked, and half the time they're wide open already) and give us tons of silver paper. I guess you couldn't go out and buy silver paper like you can now. You had to peel it off old cigarette wrappers or other kinds of packages.

Some of the people offer us cookies and fruit or a cold drink. It's a little hard getting used to all this trust and friendliness. In fact, I haven't yet. Every time my mother takes a cookie or a piece of fruit I hold my breath waiting for her to chomp on the razor blade.

Little by little it begins to dawn on me that this silver has something to do with the war. I don't know too much about it, but I do know that World War II happened in the forties. It must be going on right now. They probably melt down the silver and use it to make guns or something like that. I notice how concerned everybody is with what they call the "war effort." Wherever you look there are flags and big signs telling you to buy defense bonds or support your boys overseas or even "A slip of the lip can sink a ship." I like that one best. Everyone seems tremendously patriotic.

It's amazing. We're back home with a full carriage in less than an hour. Easiest collecting I've ever done.

"Hey," my mother says, "how about playing a little tennis down at the schoolyard? It's only over at the next block."

I don't believe it. Finally my mother actually wants to play tennis with me. "Okay by me, but I gotta tell you I'm not too great."

"Me neither."

Yeah, sure.

"C'mon, you can use Steve's racket. Wait here a sec— I'll get the stuff," she says, and shoots into the house.

Maybe I should have said no. I'm crazy about Cici, but I don't know if I'm in the mood to get blitzed at tennis. She's really going to make me look lousy. Oh, well, too late. She's back with everything already.

"Let's go," she says, and we jog off down the block.

The court is empty when we get there. Super. At least

nobody will see the massacre. As soon as we get in the court she starts apologizing, giving me a whole load of baloney about how she's only a beginner and she's pretty awful and she has no backhand and she can't serve and all that. For the first time I'm feeling a little negative about her because I hate to be conned. So I don't say much and I just let her serve.

She throws up the ball and I brace myself for her killer serve. It doesn't come the first time. Or the second time or even the third. In fact you couldn't even call what comes plopping over the net the fourth time a serve. Not only that, she doesn't have a backhand, a forehand, or anything else. She wasn't kidding. She stinks. Wow! I'm flipping out of my head because I could beat her with my eyes closed. It's almost too easy. I should just take it gentle, lob them over nice and easy right in center court. Give the kid a break. Hah!

I cream her. Three sets, all of them 6-love.

"You're terrific, Victoria. You gotta show me your serve. It's fabulous."

And so I teach my mother the very serve she taught me last summer. How does that grab you? It grabs me great. Naturally I could play all day, but by now some other kids are waiting for the court so we grab our stuff and head home.

There are some kids playing a game called "ringalevio" in the street in front of the house and they ask us to join them. Everybody's a little surprised that I don't know how to play but they show me, and after a while we switch to "kick the can" and they have to show me that too. I'm embarrassed to tell you that we even played jump rope. I haven't played that baby game in years. When that breaks up, Carolanne, my mother, and I play something called comic book. Everyone is a character from some comic.

This is obviously my mother's big game because right away she says she's somebody called Sheena of the Jungle. I'm her handmaiden and poor Carolanne gets to be the jungle. It's not exactly my favorite game, and I keep thinking that if anyone saw me playing it, I'd just die. In my time thirteen- and fourteen-year-old girls just don't play games like that. Mostly we do more mature things— like pulling our friends apart, complaining about our parents, polishing our nails, and planning the next party. Maybe we've been missing something because I've been having a fabulous time this afternoon. "Kick the can" is a super game. So what if it's little babyish?

"Felicia!" My grandmother's voice comes singing down the street. My mother pays no attention the first five times (temporary deafness runs in the family). There's not too much song left in my grandmother's voice on the sixth, seventh, and eighth yells, and by the ninth it's an angry croak followed by, "If you don't answer this second I'm coming to get you!" That does it.

"In a minute," answers my mother.

"Right now!" The command from my grandmother. It really breaks me up to hear my grandmother giving my mother orders.

"I'm coming," shouts my mother, making no move to end the game. We play for another five minutes or so, then my grandmother calls again and we beat it home. I have to admire my mom. I'd have folded after four yells and no more than two extra minutes at the end.

My grandfather is home when we get there. It's amazing but he practically looks the same as he does now, only with a little less belly. And he's still as funny. I mean he can really break me up with his jokes. Dinner is the best, though. We have chicken soup with little tiny unhatched eggs (no shells or white; they just look like mini-yokes) in it. Cici and my Uncle Steve spend half the meal arguing about who gets the extra egg. A real Nina-and-me-type situation, the kind that makes you want to throw up if you have to watch it. At one point it looks like my grandmother's going to attack them, but they get the message first and cool it. From the egg argument we move smoothly on to the lost-comic-book fight, then my Uncle Steve tells on my mother because she was late for school yesterday morning, and my mother says that my Uncle Steve hides his cigarettes under the hall radiator, and he turns purple and calls her a liar, and she says and he says and he says and she says, and I want to cry because it feels so good, just like home.

When my mother and my uncle aren't fighting, my grandmother is bugging my mother about eating. She can't leave the table until her plate is clean and she has to finish very drop of milk in her glass because everybody is starving in Armenia. My mother is a worse eater than I am, and not wanting to spend the rest of her life at the table, she secretly stuffs her broccoli under the potato shells, her meat into her napkin, and when everyone leaves the table, she feeds her milk to the geraniums. I have to admit my mother did learn something as a kid. She never bugs Nina and me about eating. She's definitely the type to; because she hassles us about everything else, but I guess she remembers how terrible it was for her. Anyhow, that business with the potato skins was pretty sharp.

After dinner I pull a fast one on everyone. I pretend I called my mother and that she said I can stay for the weekend. Of course Cici is delighted (sometimes it feels more natural to call her Cici and not "my mother") that I can go to the party with her. Me too. And besides, it gives me an extra day to come up with a reason for never going home. Oh, boy, that's going to be a beaut.

## Twelve

It takes us almost two hours to dress for the party. We try on every dress in her closet. She wouldn't dream of wearing pants to a party—I mean we really get dressed up like for a wedding or something. Naturally we end up wearing the same peasant outfits we said we were going to wear in the first place. The rest of her wardrobe is right where it fell on the floor.

At some point my grandmother comes in and suggests we tidy up a bit.

"This room looks like a cyclone hit it." Guess who's talking. "Don't you dare move from here until every stitch of clothing is picked up and put away. How many times do I have to tell you . . ." and so on and so on.

We work pretty fast and most of the clothes are picked up during the cyclone part of the speech, and by the time my grandmother finishes up with how God forbid some stranger should walk into the room and see such a mess (I guess it's the same stranger my mother's always warning about in my own life who'll look away in disgust at my torn underwear when I've been in a horrible accident), we've folded everything and put it away. Not only that, we're dressed and ready to go.

We get to the party around eight and most everyone is there. I get to meet Janet Foley of the big boobs, and of course grungy Betty and snobby Joyce are there, and some absolutely horrendous boys who are even shorter than the boys in my class, which practically makes them midgets. Nice.

We play the usual games—Spin the Bottle, Post Office, and a lights-out-free-for-all. Some joker turns the lights on unexpectedly and a creep named Ralph is caught with his hand under Janet's sweater. She's really too much. She doesn't even look embarrassed. Mostly the boys hang out on one side of the room (everyone calls it a "finished basement") yakking and combing their hair so it stands four inches high off their foreheads, and the girls giggle on the other side. Except for the people it's exactly the same as all the parties I've ever gone to—a bummer.

One of the boys comes up with the bright idea that we should dance, so they put one of those old 78 r.p.m. records on the stereo, which is called a Victrola. It's really funky music and you should see the gross dance they do to it. It's called a jitterbug or sometimes a lindy, and it's wild. Looks like the whole thing is how far the guy can throw his partner out and then as soon as she starts coming back he gives her another shove that either sends her spinning in nice circles or flying through the wall. Definitely not my bag. Everybody dies when Frank Sinatra comes on. Actually he sounds pretty good if you could just listen. But you gotta dance and that's the worst. I dance with one creep and he holds me so close I think I'm going to end up behind him. It makes you feel very uncomfortable feeling so much of a boy's body. At least it does me. The next one who asks me to dance I tell him I can't because of my hammertoes. I don't even know what that is, but it sounds heavy and it's a sure turn-off.

The weirdest thing, though, is watching my own mother kissing boys, especially this guy Danny. I think she really likes him. I'm not saying he's grotesque or anything like that, but he certainly doesn't hold a candle to my father. Naturally my dad isn't here because they didn't even meet till my mother was twenty-one. It would really be great seeing them both together. But right now, if my calculations are right, he's in this dinky little burg called Ypsilanti. Too bad.

I have to admit it sort of bothers me a teeny bit seeing how much she likes this Danny jerk.

"Hey, Victoria." It's my mother pulling me aside. "What do you think?

"About the party?"

"Parties are all the same. I mean what do you think about Danny?"

"That freak? Ugh, he's some weirdo. I mean he is the grossest, grungiest, most horrendous creep I've ever seen. Mr. Instant Turn-off." And just so there's not even a pinpoint of room for misunderstanding, I let out with a real Academy Award "Yiiiich!"

My mother's face drops down to her knees and you can see that she's really knocked out by my reaction. I know it's a lousy thing to do but I have to look out for my own welfare, don't I? I mean, I am definitely not taking any chances that I'll end up with him for a father. I mean, no way. For one thing, he thinks he's hot stuff, and for another he's probably a real bomb at Coney Island, and for a third, he's much too short.

Cici couldn't have been too crazy about him anyway because she sort of turns off after she hears my reaction. See that? I may have had a hand in my own destiny. Either that or I just blitzed some poor guy's big night. Whatever, the party turns out to be a real downer for me. Except for the big showoffs slinging each other around in this grotesque jitterbug that they do, hardly anybody dances or anything. Just a whole load of kissing games which wouldn't be such a drag if there was someone worth kissing. Which, of course, there isn't. And if that isn't bad enough, there's this little snook, this really jerky asshole, who actually makes an "ugh" face when he has to kiss me. Can you imagine? I mean this nobody, this little acne pimple— God, sometimes I wonder why I expose myself to these dumb parties. Always, every time, they turn out to be bombs. So why am I always so anxious to go?

I can't wait for this one to end. Luckily it's not too long because at about ten to eleven Cici pulls me over to the side and says we have to go home. We thread our way through the kissers and gropers and find our way out to the street.

"Sorry for the big rush," Cici says.

"Forget it. You did me a favor."

"They're always a big letdown, aren't they?"

"You know it!" Will you look at that? It's incredible how much we think alike. What happened to change her so much?

On the way home she tells me the bad news. At least I think it's bad news. She got a note from Ted saying that he has the test and for her to meet him on the corner at eleven-thirty tonight. I'm beginning to get very nervous, but Cici looks cool.

The minute we get home she rushes me up to the bedroom. As soon as she closes the door I see that kooky expression come over her face. It's sort of half grin and half trouble, something like a wink, and it means another caper. I don't know if I'm up to a Woolworth-type adventure, but I'm certainly not going to let my own mother risk her neck alone, so like it or not I'm in it. I feed her the right question because I see she's dying to tell me her plans.

"How are we going to get out to meet Ted?"

"It's a snap," she says, and we're off and running. "First thing we do is stuff the beds to look like we're sleeping in case my parents look in. They never do, but you know me, I like to be cautious."

If she's being careful, it's going to be more horrendous than I thought.

"Then all we do is slip out that window," she says, pointing to the one that leads onto a porch, "and slide down that tree and that's all there is to it."

Maybe it's not so horrendous. From the easy way she makes it sound she's probably done it millions of times before. I look out the window but I don't see any tree. It's very dark. I can make out the porch railing and what looks like plain emptiness past that except for a skinny stick poking up in the far corner. Oh, no!

"That thing over there isn't the tree, is it?"

"Right."

I don't know why I bother to ask such a dumb question when I know the answer all along. "I kind of thought it would be bigger," I say nervously.

"It used to be when it was alive."

No way to stop these old air vents from opening in my stomach. A dead dried-out stick that's surely going to snap the minute I step on it. I'm probably beginning to look a little green because suddenly my mother is very concerned.

"Hey, don't worry. It makes it even easier to slide down without the leaves in your way. Besides, it's only two stories and most of the time you can hang on to the edge of the porch."

Funny thing is most people think I'm pretty gutsy at home, but next to my mother I'm a scaredy cat. I'm being dumb. Like I said, she's probably done it a million times before.

"I'll be all right," I stammer. "It's just—you know, the first time it's kind of scary."

"I understand. Don't feel embarrassed. It's the first for me too and I'm probably just as scared."

"You mean you never did this before?"

"You kidding?"

"But all that business about sliding down and hanging on to the edge . . ."

"Just a matter of all the long and careful planning I've been doing . . ."

I'm relieved. I know for a fact that my mother is a fantastically responsible person. Once she gets involved in a project she can spend weeks just putting together the proper approach. She's highly organized, and I've put myself in her hands many times in almost fourteen years so I guess I can take a chance again.

" . . . all the way home."

"What 'all the way home'?" I guess I wasn't listening.

"That's when I worked the plan out."

All the way home! The party was a half a block away. I take another look at the tree and it's even skinnier than before. Ah, well, I have no choice anyway. I'm certainly not going to let her meet this creep alone.

"Count me in." The sacrifices we make for our parents.

"Great. Watch, I'll show you how to do the beds." And she starts rolling up a blanket. When it's about the size of a four-year-old, she slides it under the covers, punches a spot in the pillow and says, "There!" She's got what looks like a full-grown dwarf all squinched up in 20-degree weather in the middle of December. The fact that it's the end of May and 75 degrees could cause a

credibility gap just big enough for a grandmother to fall
into, but I guess it's no time to be picky so I just shut
up and start rolling. Besides the bed is nothing compared
to that tree.

# Thirteen

"That's perfect, Victoria," my mother says, inspecting my handiwork and sounding strangely like my mother. This whole thing is so weird. Anyway, she opens the window and motions me to follow as she starts crawling out onto the porch. She whispers that it's better if we stay low just in case her brother Steve is looking. One of his windows faces the porch too. I answer, "Far out!" and she answers, "Only about ten feet."

It's a warm velvety night and it feels like you're in the country except that there are no country sounds. It's perfectly still and silent except for us squeaking our way across the porch. This is about the most terrifying thing I've ever done in my life. I went to summer camps for years and we always used to sneak out at night to meet the boys, but that was different. The whole camp thing was sort of fake, a let's-pretend world where playing tricks like frenching beds and sneaking out was expected, even laughed at. But this is the real world and what we're doing is no trick—it's dishonest. We're not just fooling around—we're sneaking out to buy stolen property, which is illegal, so that my mother can cheat on a test, which is immoral. And if we get caught, they're not going to just dock us from next week's social. It could be bad news for my mother. Not only won't she graduate but she'll surely get kicked out of school. And maybe worse. I wish I could stop her.

My face is dripping wet just thinking about the terrible things that could happen to her. I mean, the ground seems awfully far away. And that stupid twig of a tree doesn't help either. In fact the combinations of awfuls is making me very queasy. I wish I had some gum. I have some in my bag but that's in the room. This is getting to be an emergency.

"Cici," I whisper poking her in the back lightly. "I got to have some gum. Don't move. I'll be back in a sec."

"Wait," she says reaching into her pocket. "I've got some right here." And she hands me the biggest ball of bubble gum I've ever seen. I pop the gum in my mouth and stuff the paper in my pocket. Just in time. It's almost impossible to chew this enormous glob of gum but it does the trick.

"I'll go first, then I can help you from the bottom," Cici says. "Now remember, hang on to the porch as long as you can. Okay?" And with that my mother leaps over the railing and starts to slide down the tree as easy as pie. The tree bends dangerously back and forth, but she's on the ground before it can break. Besides, I know it's waiting for me before it does its snap, crackle, and plop number. I know I can easily come up with four hundred fantastic reasons for shooting back into the house, but they all fall apart when I think about my mother's terrible predicament and that I'm probably the only person in the whole world who can help her. I don't even know how I can do that, but I know I have to try, so I kick off my clogs and start to climb over the rickety wooden railing. A splinter cuts into my palm and a sensible voice inside my brain reminds me that I am not, after all, my mother's keeper. But it's too late, I'm already on the skinny outside rim of the porch and not about to risk climbing back over the rail again. Besides I think it's my brother's keeper anyway. Without loosening my grip on the railing, I wrap my legs around the tree branch and it starts zinging back and forth like a rubber band. I can feel it's going to snap if I put all my weight on it, so I let my hands slide down the spokes of the railing as far as they can while I lower my legs down the tree. It's still too high for me to jump. My mother is encouraging me from the ground in whispers.

"It's okay, you can let go of the porch now and just slide down. I'll grab you before you hit the ground."

It's not okay because I can't let go. My legs keep slipping down the tree, stretching my body till it feels like my arms are going to pull right out of their sockets. Still, it's like my hands are welded to the porch. I can't make them let go.

Suddenly there's a wrenching sound of wood splitting and I go hurtling down the tree. In the blur I see my mother making a grab for me but I'm going too fast and too hard. In a whoosh my bare feet whack into the ground and I go sprawling. We both hold our breath and wait for lights to go on and windows to open. But nothing happens. I think I'm okay; at least I can move everything. Incredibly, the tree is in one piece, but I'm still clutching part of the railing in my hands.

"Wow, you really came flying. Are you hurt?" My mother helps me up, prying the spokes out of my hands and brushing off the twigs and dirt.

"Uh-huh. Just a splinter in my hand and some scrapes, but I made a mess of that railing. I'm really sorry."

"Forget it. Nobody ever uses that porch anyway. Are you sure you still want to come with me?"

"Absolutely." Anything is better than going back up that tree again.

"Okay, then let's go. Ted's going to be waiting on the corner. Hey, your shoes!"

Forget it. I wouldn't go back for my feet, much less my shoes. But I don't want her to think I'm a complete coward, so I tell her that I left my clogs because they're too noisy.

"Good idea," she says. "Let's go," and she leads the way. We tiptoe along the side of the house, silently, hunched over like cat thieves. My mother goes down the front steps to the street and I follow behind her closer than her shadow. Even from the middle of the block we can see Ted's car (my mother calls it a "hot rod") parked at the corner. There's enough light from the streetlight to see that he's really gross, especially his hair. The length isn't so bad, but he has this big high loopy pompadour in front and then the hair laps over at the back of his head. Gorgeous.

Right away I can see he thinks he's too cool for words. Funny thing about my mother. She's certainly no jerk—I mean she really knows her way around and nothing seems to scare her and in most ways I feel very dependent on her, but still she sometimes seems a little naïve, much too trusting. Like with this creep. I wouldn't trust this worm no how. One look and you can see how spaced out he is.

First thing Ted says when we get up to the car is, "What'd you bring her for?" Meaning me.

"Why shouldn't I?" my mother says, giving him sneer for sneer. "She's a very good friend and besides I told her everything."

"Dumb broad," he says. Oh, I really love this guy. "Get in," he says to my mother, motioning to the seat next to him. "You"—pointing to me—"get in the back."

"Just a minute." When my mother uses that tone— watch out! "Who do you think you're pushing around, Mr. Hot Shot?" C'mon, *Ma*! "Why do we have to get in your stupid car anyway? Just give me the paper and I'll give you the money. We're not looking for a joyride, especially not with you.''

''You want the test? Get in the car.''

''What for?''

'' 'Cause I have to get it, that's what for.''

''Why didn't you bring it with you? Look, jerko, I'm not supposed to be out now. If my parents find out they'll kill me.''

''That's your tough luck. You didn't think I'd be dumb enough to risk getting caught with the goods.''

I may be wrong but I think this jerk sees too many movies. Either that or he's got something up his sleeve.

''It's not exactly the Hope diamond,'' says my mother fairly reasonably. ''It's just a little science test that nobody but me cares about. So why don't you just get it now and let's get this thing over with.''

''I just finished telling you I don't have it with me.''

''Oh, damn! Come on, Victoria, let's go with Humphrey Bogart or whoever he is, or we'll never get the damn thing tonight.''

And we both get in the front seat. Humphrey Bogart isn't too happy with the arrangement. It's obvious, now that the door is closed, that a lot of his spaced-out look and great gangster style is plain old beer. The car reeks of it.

''Where are we going?'' I ask, because I can't sit like a dummy, and besides I want to make sure he's awake.

''None of your business.'' What a charmer.

We drive around for fifteen minutes, and even though I don't know where I am, still I get the impression that we're going in one big circle. All the time we're riding, Ted doesn't say a word, but you can see he's very busy planning something. Finally he seems to make up his mind and pulls over to the side of the street in front of an iron

gate. I'm certain we passed this same place a few minutes
ago. I give my mother a tiny poke in the side and whisper,
"What's up?" But she just shrugs. So we sit and wait.
Obviously Ted has something on his mind but he doesn't
seem to have the nerve to do it. Finally he reaches into the
back seat and comes up with a bottle of beer, gulps down
half of it, and offers us the rest. We both say no thanks.
He's annoyed and polishes off the rest of the bottle and
tosses it out the window. Pig.

"Your friend gets out here," he announces. Obviously
that's what he was working up his nerve for. Well, he
wasted his time. He must be nuts if he thinks I'm going to
let him put me out in the middle of nowhere at midnight.

"Forget it," my mother snaps back. "She stays with
me." Wonderful mother.

"I'm not turning over anything with a witness. You
want to forget the whole deal?"

"I told you she knows all about it so what difference
does it make if she sees it?"

"It makes a difference to me. You don't like it? Lump
it."

"Look, I gotta have that test."

"Then tell your friend to get out."

"Hey, wait a minute!" I thought I'd never open my
mouth. "You can't shove me out like that. I don't even
know where I am. How am I going to find my way
home?" I probably sound like I'm whining, but I don't
care.

"Nobody said you had to find your way anywhere," the
freak says, capturing my whine perfectly. "Just get out of
the car and wait right here while we drive around the block
and close the deal."

"How long will it take?" I don't know why I ask.
Twenty seconds would be too long.

"I don't know—give us ten, fifteen minutes."

"But it's not safe to stand here alone." I turn to my mother for support.

"It's all right," says my wonderful mother, the rat traitor. "Nobody's around."

That's just it. Nobody's around. What's the matter with her, anyway? People don't just stand out on empty streets late at night all alone. Especially a girl my age. What's happening? At home she goes berserk when I want to take a bus after dark.

"Come on, you're holding up the works," says Mr. Vomit, who obviously can't wait to get my mother alone in the car.

But I can't bring myself to move.

"Don't worry." My mother tries to reassure me. "I'll make it fast. You'll see, we'll be back in less than five minutes."

I'm trapped. I can't ruin everything for my mother just because I'm scared of the dark, so I have no choice. I open the door and sit there staring out.

"Move it!" This is so grossly unfair, but what can I do? I get out of the car, slam the door, and before I can even turn around I hear the car screech away.

Here I am, totally alone, not just on this street but in the whole world. I back up against an iron gate. It's pretty dark, but if I stay perfectly still maybe they'll think I'm just a big lump in the gate. They, of course, are the stealers, rapers, muggers, and murderers that my mother has been warning me about since before I can remember. Those same monsters she's throwing me out to tonight.

It's absolutely silent on the street and, with the trees tunneling the entire block, inky black. No cars pass. I wait, straining my eyes to catch a glimpse of Ted's car coming around the corner. But there's nothing but dark emptiness down there. Then something, maybe a cat or a squirrel, darts out in front of me and the lump on the gate leaps a mile. A dog howls somewhere in one of the houses down at the far end of the block and the numbness in my head begins to subside enough for me to make out some night sounds, crickets and things like that. There's a slight breeze that rustles the leaves and carries the pleasant odor of fresh-cut grass. My mother's probably right. I'll be okay. Things were different in the forties, much quieter and safer, and you didn't have to worry about being out alone at night.

In fact, I'm probably safer alone in the street right now than she is in the car trying to fight off that moron. It feels like at least five minutes (more like five hours) have passed and they should be coming around the corner any second. By the time I count to 46 (my new lucky number) the glare from their headlights should be visible. One, two, three . . . I'll close my eyes and open them at 46 . . . 45678910111213141516 . . .

Oh my God!

There's a man. I can just make him out way down at the end of the street! And he's coming right toward me. I can't tell if he's young or old but he looks big—I mean huge, tall, and fat. I can't let myself jump to conclusions, but the odds are against me. I mean, sure he could be a plain old nice man, or he could be a mugger, stealer, rapist, or murderer. That's what I mean, there's only one little chance in four that he's okay. It's four to one against me. I'm in big trouble. He's walking pretty fast. I've already jumped to conclusions, so now I gotta make up my mind . . . if I run I've still got a good head start. But where am I going to run to? I don't even know where I am, and then how will my mother find me? Maybe if I stand perfectly still he won't see me. That's dumb. He'd have to be blind not to spot me. I've got to stay cool. Oooh, I think he just spotted me. He hesitates for just a second, and now he's walking slower than before.

Now that he's closer I can see that he's certainly not a priest. If that car doesn't come by the time he gets up to the tree about fifteen feet away from me, I'm going to start screaming and running and pounding on doors and everything. I don't care. He's got another ten seconds.

Where is that car!

But it's still black down at the corner, and now he's right smack in front of me. He stops. My fingers squeeze around the rungs of the gate behind me. It's too late to run. I'll just hang onto the gate and scream and kick. . . .

"Hello, young lady."

"Hello," I say before I can stop myself. Would you believe how well trained I am? I'm even polite to my own killer. He smiles and I can feel my face freeze in terror.

"Is there anything wrong?" he asks, trying to pass himself off as a terrific person just interested in my welfare.

"My, what's a young lady like you doing out this late?" He's still pretending he's not a killer, but I'm not fooled. It's just a matter of time before he attacks me. I've gotta do something!

"Are you lost?"

"No, sir. Absolutely not. The soldiers are right around the corner."

"Soldiers?"

"Out collecting silver. Hundreds of them. Pushing their doll carriages."

Where *is* that car!

He looks at me hard for a moment. "Well," he finally says, "I'm sure the soldiers are watching out for you. But look, I live just up that block, in that white house over there. Why don't you come home and my wife will make some cocoa and we can call your parents and they can come and pick you up.''

Me? Go in that house with this old smoothie? No way. Then I see it out of the corner of my eye. The car. It swings into the block and here it comes.

''Speak of the devil,'' I blurt to the man. ''Here come my folks now.'' The car pulls up and Ted and Cici peer out. ''Hi, Mom,'' I practically yell as I pile into the car. ''Step on it, Dad, the general's waiting.'' As the car pulls away, I wave at the man and shout, ''Remember the Maine!''

''What was that all about?'' Naturally they're both really confused. Then my mother says, ''Am I supposed to be your mother?'' I just shrug my shoulders and laugh. I mean, what do you do with that kind of question?

Then I tell them about my narrow escape. But all Cici does is say, ''You're loony. This is the safest neighborhood in the world.'' She gives Ted a hate stare. ''On the street, anyway. It can get a little dangerous inside a car.'' I start to argue and rattle on about knifers and muggers and all, but Cici's not really listening, and I can see she's upset about something so I lean over and whisper to her, ''What's up?''

''Fink over here,'' she says good and loud, ''decided that two dollars isn't enough, especially since he found out there are no fringe benefits.''

''Fringe benefits?''

''He expected me to put out,'' she says, really zinging it to Ted whose ears turn a brilliant scarlet. Suddenly he gets real busy staring straight ahead and concentrating so hard he could be driving on a tightrope. ''And when I smacked him,'' my mother continues, ''he called the whole deal off.''

I glare daggers at him. Propositioning my own teen-age mother! I could kill him right then and there.

"Ten bucks," he suddenly says, "that's the price. Take it or leave it." He pulls up in front of my mother's house.

"Cici." I poke my mother. "I want to talk to you for a sec."

"Sure thing, Victoria, right after I tell this bum a few little things that are on my mind."

"Forget it. The deal's off, period," Ted snarls. He's hot to leave.

"You probably never even had the blasted test anyhow."

"That's what you think," he says, and reaches into the glove compartment and pulls out what looks like a mimeographed page.

"Well, it doesn't make any difference, I haven't got ten dollars no how."

"Cici." I'm pulling at her sleeve, trying to get her out of the car so I can talk to her before she starts to unload on Ted, which she is going to do any second.

"First thing you can do"—she's so close she looks like she's going to bite his nose off—"is drop dead! Then . . ."

"Cici . . ." Now I'm practically dragging her out of the car. "It's important."

"I'm coming." But she's not, so I whisper that I can lend her some of the money. That makes her practically jump out of the car.

"You can? Neato! How much?"

"I have six dollars"—it's the emergency money my mother gave me, so in a crazy way it's hers already—"and with your two that's eight. Ask him, maybe he'll settle for that."

"Wait a minute. It's really terrif, but I don't know when I could pay you back. It would take me forever to save six dollars. I get thirty-five cents allowance, and even if I save the whole thing plus baby-sitting—I have this steady job two hours a week, that's fifty cents, plus things like deposit bottles and . . .''

"Forget it. I don't need it back for ages."

"You're really sensational, and don't worry 'cause I'll pay you back even if it takes a year. Gee, thanks a million. Really, I . . .''

"You better ask the creep if he'll take eight instead of ten. You never know with him, he's so gross."

"Okay, wait, here." And she goes over to the car and leans in the window. I can hear him giving her a really hard time. That's a lot of money to turn down, considering he's already done all the risky work—stealing it, I mean. I've got a feeling something's fishy. After a couple of minutes my mother comes back, really dragging.

"He says no dice. Ten or nothing."

"What are you going to do?"

"There's one last thing, but I hate to . . ."

"What is it?"

"A charity box. Oh, God, it's just terrible even to think of such a thing."

"You mean like a church?"

"Not exactly. It's the USO. You know, they entertain the troops and things like that."

"That doesn't sound much like a charity. I mean, it's not something serious like cancer or starving children."

"But it's the war effort, and I've collected from a lot of people, and besides the soldiers really need it, and I don't know . . .''

"How much have you got?"

"Oh, probably four or five dollars. I don't know exactly—it's in a sealed box."

"You only need two dollars. You can pay that back in a month." I know I was the one who was against the whole idea from the beginning, but now that I'm really into it I see we have to go all the way. After all, nobody wants to see their own mother go through the disgrace of being left back. Worse than that, not graduate. Especially when your mother's such a terrific person. That's heavy stuff—not graduating, I mean. When I weigh that against some junky old song and dance routine, I mean, like there's no choice. So here I am, trying to convince my mother that it's all right for her to steal from a charity box to buy answers from a moral degenerate to a stolen test. Super. Next thing you know we'll be holding up gas stations. Of course, I do have an advantage. I happen to know that even without that two dollars, we won the war and there's still a USO.

"All you do is send the money in anonymously. Nobody will ever know." I guess I'm pressing, but I want her to pass that stupid old test. Turns out that she doesn't need much convincing.

"Okay," she tells Ted, "I'll give you the ten dollars." And it's really weird, but I think he looks a little disappointed. I told you I think something's screwy. "Except," she says, "I have to get the money from my room, so in the meantime you give the test to Victoria to hold and you can hold the eight dollars."

Reluctantly Ted folds the test tightly in half, then in quarters, and hands it to me.

"Thanks, sport." I can't resist the dig.

"C'mon, Victoria," my mother says, grabbing my arm. "Let's go."

"Hey, wait a minute!" The would-be defiler of my mother's purity grabs my other arm. "Where's she going with that test?"

"She's gotta come with me. I need her help getting up the tree."

"What tree?"

"The one to the porch. That's the only way I can get back into the house."

"Yeah, well, I'm coming too."

"Suit yourself. C'mon, Victoria." And the three of us sneak up the front steps and around to the back of the house. The thought of going back up that tree, especially barefooted, turns my stomach. I don't know how I'm going to get back in, but I'm not going to worry about it now. Of course, my mother makes it look like a snap the way she shimmies up the tree and with one flying leap skims over the railing and lands silently on the porch. Even jerko is impressed. She ducks down and crawls along the porch and into the open window.

## *Fourteen*

Watching her now reminds me how once, about two years ago, we were on a picnic with two other families in some park on Staten Island, and I don't know why, but everybody (the adults anyway) was kidding around and daring each other to do all sorts of crazy things like swinging from monkey bars and climbing trees. I remember that my mother climbed higher than anybody else, so high that I began to get a little worried. Everyone else thought it was hysterical, but it seemed kind of peculiar, even a little embarrassing to me. Now that I consider it, I guess it was kind of unfair of me to be embarrassed. After all, just because you've got children doesn't mean you're nothing but a mother. I'm hopeless when it comes to my mother. Everything about her is either embarrassing, irritating, or just plain confusing. I don't know why I can't just say she's a super climber and let it go at that.

Anyway, here's Ted and me waiting around for her, kind of kicking the dirt and not talking. By now he knows I can't stand his guts and I'm sure he feels the same way about me. He probably thinks I screwed up his big chance with my mother. Little does he know he never had one.

It's very quiet except for a funny scraping sound every few seconds. It seems to be coming from the house. There it goes again. I've heard that sound before but I can't think

where. It's kind of like when you shake . . . of course!
She's shaking the charity box, trying to get the coins out. I
should have told her to stick a knife in the slot and let the
coins slide out on it. It always works on Nina's piggy
bank. The sound stops and I catch a glimpse of my mother's
head coming out the window. She's across the porch and
at the railing before I can tell her to get a knife. She clears
the railing and fairly glides down the tree and lands with a
clink of the coin box.

"I've been shaking this thing like mad and all I got out
is fourteen cents. At this rate it'll take me all week."
She's still shaking the box furiously.

"Take it easy," I say, "I can do it. All I need's a
knife."

"They'd hear me for sure if I tried to get to the kitchen,"
my mother says.

"How about if we break it?"

"No good. It's metal."

All this time the creep has been real quiet. Finally he
says, "Well, looks like we'll have to forget the whole
thing." And he starts to walk away.

"Hey, wait a minute," my mother says, grabbing him
by the sleeve. I still can't get over how anxious he is to
drop a ten-dollar deal. That really throws me.

"What do you want?" He sounds really mean now.

"Your pocketknife."

"Who says I have one?"

For a second my mother doesn't answer. She just nar-
rows her eyes and stares at him real hard. Just exactly like
she does when she catches me trying to hide something. "I
do." And she's practically tapping her foot. He hasn't got
a chance and he knows it!

"Let's have it," my mother commands, and Ted reaches

into his side pocket and takes out one of those gigantic Boy Scout knives.

"Gimme the biggest blade you've got." I try to sound like my mother. He opens the knife instantly and hands it to me. Obviously he's one of those jerks who responds automatically when you give him an order. I wish we had known that before. Could have saved ourselves a lot of trouble. Anyway I get to work pushing the knife blade into the opening at the top of the box, and after a couple of experienced shakes the coins start to slide down the knife and into my lap. It couldn't be easier and in less than three minutes I've got exactly two dollars in front of me. My mother is really pleased.

"You're really a pro, Victoria. You saved my life. Thanks. I'll never forget you."

That's the nicest thing my mother ever said to me. And right this second I think I love her more than I ever loved her in my whole life. I'm so glad I could do something so important for her. It makes me feel so puffed up I could explode. Now if only I didn't have to climb back up that tree, life would be close to perfect.

"Okay," my mother says, handing Ted the two dollars in change. "That makes ten bucks even, right?"

"Yeah."

"The deal is closed, right?"

"Yeah," the submoron grunts again.

"In that case, I'd like to tell you something."

"Don't bother."

"You're a number-one bastard."

"Up yours."

"Drop dead!"

"TS." And he starts to leave. It's a waste of time to insult jerks like Ted. Like talking at a toad.

"Hey, wait a minute," my mother calls after him. "You gotta help Victoria up the tree."

"Fat chance. Why should I help her?"

"Because," my mother says, "if you don't we'll never get back, and then we're certain to get caught, and if we do, guess who's going to get found out too. That's why."

Obviously the reason is good enough because he comes back. My mother scoots up the tree and over the railing.

"Victoria, you start up the tree and I'll grab you when you get close to the rim of the porch, okay?"

I know I've said a million times how terrified I feel about climbing that tree, but this time the vibes are overpowering. I just know it's going to snap. I know it, but what can I do? I have to get up to that room or I'll blow the whole plan. Mr. Obnoxious puts his hands together to make a step for me. I've never been terrifically graceful, but in terror I'm a complete klutz. It takes me four tries before I can even get onto the tree. Now I have one foot wrapped around the trunk and one foot still on Ted's hands. I get the sinking feeling that I may stay this way forever.

"C'mon, Victoria, just a little higher and I can reach your hand." My mother is trying to be encouraging, but I can't get a firm hold on the tree in my bare feet, and that splinter in my hand is killing me so I can't get a good grip on the branch. I try to take my foot out of Ted's hands and for a second I do, but then panic hits when he starts to move away and I kick out and my foot lands in his face.

"Hey!" he says pretty loud. "What're you doing!" And he shoves my foot hard and my whole body goes swaying to one side and the tree goes with it and . . . aiii . . . it's . . . "Help!" I scream as the tree snaps and I go sprawling all over Ted, who's knocked down under me, luckily breaking my fall. Two dollars' worth of change goes flying all over the ground.

"Victoria!" my mother shouts from the porch. "Are you okay?" And she leaps over the railing, lowers herself onto the edge of the porch until she's hanging by her fingertips, then lets go, dropping at least ten feet. She hits the ground lightly and rolls over to where I'm still flat out on top of Ted.

Suddenly, from no place, bright searchlights blast us from all directions, bouncing and leaping over the three of us. In panic we all roll in different directions and scramble to our feet, trying to jump away from the blinding glare. One of the lights lands on me and I stop dead, pinned in the center. I can't see who's at the other end, but I can see that they've nailed my mother too. I don't see Ted.

"Okay, you kids, don't move!" It's a man, barking out the command in a no-kidding voice. We don't kid around. In fact, we don't move an inch. At the sound of his voice lights go on all over my mother's house and the house next door. Now the searchlights come closer and I can make out two men. I think to myself: Shit! They're policemen and they've got guns and—you won't believe this, but they're pointing them at us!

## Fifteen

"Please, Officer, don't shoot. We live here," my mother says, reaching out and taking my hand like I was her child and she was going to protect me. Unreal!

"What are you doing here?" one of them says, and this time it's more of a real question than a command, and before we can even answer they put their guns back in their holsters and lower the lights from our faces.

"We didn't know it was so late . . . we were just . . . well . . . we were . . ." My mother's stumbling so I jump in.

" . . . camping out."

"Yeah, that's right, you know, in the great outdoors, under the stars and all that . . ." She's wasting her time because by now the whole family's out of the house along with all the next-door neighbors, and even the people two and three houses down have turned on their lights and opened their windows. The jig's up, but that doesn't stop dear old Mom. She just rambles on and on about the virtues of life on the prairie (I think she said prairie but it doesn't make any difference, I'm the only one listening). All the while the two policemen are looking around, examining the money on the ground and the charity box propped up against the tree. That's when I spot the test paper. It's only about three feet from me. Nonchalantly I sort of slide over to the spot and reach down to pick it up, but one of the cops, a big fat guy, is too fast for me. He grabs it first.

"My God! What happened! Felicia, are you all right? What's happening?" By now my grandmother is out of the house and rushing toward us, grabbing this way and that way at her half-on robe.

"It's okay, Mommy, I can explain." But nobody gives her a chance. My grandfather and grandmother are all over us in a second, all concerned, asking a million questions like, "What's going on? What happened? Are you hurt? Did you fall? Why? Who? What?" And no stopping for explanations, which is just as well because the ony explanation we have isn't so hot.

Cici keeps saying that we're all right, we're fine, nobody's hurt, and all that. "I can explain if you just wait a minute, I'll tell you the whole thing."

But that still doesn't seem to calm my grandmother. "I don't understand," she says. "It's the middle of the night. What are you doing in the back yard? Why aren't you in bed?" And she turns to my grandfather like he knows the whole story. "What's going on here, Ned?"

"We'll find out as soon as we let the girls get a word in, dear, and I suggest we do it inside." My grandfather sensibly takes charge, just like he always does. "We'll all go in the house and sit down calmly and talk. Come on, girls." And he starts to lead us into the house.

"One minute, please, people." One of the policemen stops us. "We gotta straighten a few things out first. We got a call on breaking and entering from a Mr."—the cop checks his notebook—"a Mr. Owens of 108-67 88th Road."

"That's me, Officer," says one of the neighbors, looking very embarrassed as he pushes his way through what now must be a crowd of about ten or so curious neighbors.

"I made that call. Sorry, Ned," he says to my grandfather, "but it looked like robbers to me."

"You did the right thing, Tom. Thank heavens it was only the girls. But thanks anyway. We appreciate your trying to help." And my grandfather shakes Tom's hand just to show that he really is grateful. My grandfather's good that way. He always tries to make people feel they've done the right thing, made the right choice. He's always been so wise.

The police take down some names and unimportant things like addresses and such, and then one of them says to my grandparents, "Looks like you people can handle this yourselves." And my grandparents agree and thank them, and it's all so nice and pleasant that I almost forget that we're about to have our heads chopped off or something equally horrendous when they find out what really happened.

Just as the police turn to leave, the fat one hands my grandfather the test paper. "You better take a look at this." Then my grandfather does a weird thing. He hands the paper to my mother without even unfolding it.

The police leave and the neighbors, seeing that the show is over for the night, start to drift into their houses. And then it hits me. Where's Ted!

I look behind me and all around but he's not there. I see the surprised expression on my mother's face and I know that she's thinking the same thing. The rat's disappeared. He must have slipped away in all the confusion. And with our eight dollars too! What a bummer.

"Maybe you girls had better pick up that money before you come in," says my grandfather. Meanwhile my grandmother switches on the outside lights so we can see better. They wait until we've retrieved most of the two dollars, then my grandfather tells us to come inside and we can get anything we've missed in the morning.

"We're missing almost twenty cents." My mother is trying to stall. "Maybe I should get my flashlight and we'll look around a little longer." Something like about three or four weeks is probably what she has in mind but my grandfather's not buying it and picks up the charity box and says he wants us both in the living room this minute and that's that.

It really freaks me out to hear my grandfather giving orders like that. I mean, when he's my real grandfather, years and years from now, he hardly ever gets angry at anyone, especially my mother or me. It's a part of him I never saw and it really makes me nervous. Everyone troops into the house after him. He leads me right into the living room, and I can see that my mother's even more nervous than I am and I don't blame her. Boy, it's really all over for her. I wish I could help her, but I can't think of any way.

My grandparents, looking very glum, take the two big easy chairs, and my mother and I squeeze together as close as possible in the center of the gigantic couch directly facing them. Uncle Steve plops himself down on the floor between the four of us so he doesn't miss a thing. Nice to know someone is enjoying himself. I'm making a mental note to really hate him in the future or the past or whatever.

"Well, go on, what happened?" Uncle Steve says, practically drooling at the mouth.

"That'll be enough, Steven. If you want to stay, I don't want to hear another word out of you. Is that clear?"

Hooray for you, Grandma!

And then she snaps out another few mother phrases that shut him up instantly. I think he'd rather die than miss this.

"All right, Felicia," says my grandfather, and you can see he's bracing himself for the worst, which is only about half as bad as he's going to get. "Start at the beginning."

There's a terrible silence for about thirty seconds, then my mother says, "Uhhh . . . ," takes a deep breath, and looks at me.

Oh my God! I have to do something. She's counting on me.

"It was my fault." I leap in. "I mean, well, I met this boy at the party and I was . . . I was sneaking out to see him, and then Cici . . . I mean, Felicia . . ." I don't know what I'm saving, but it doesn't matter because nobody's buying it anyhow.

"Thanks, anyway, Victoria." My mother gives me the tiniest of smiles. "But I want it to be over. . . ." And then practically pleading, "I can't stand how awful it makes me feel."

I should have known. The way she acted at the time it didn't seem to bother her that much, but I should have guessed how much agony she was going through just from how sick it made me feel inside.

"Mommy." She turns to my grandmother, and you can barely hear her. "I've never been so ashamed of anything in my whole life. It's terrible. . . ."

Now she buries her face in her hands, and all I want to do is put my arms around her and hug her tight. But then, all by herself, she sort of pulls herself together, and you can see she's determined to get it over with once and for all.

And she does.

Even Uncle Steve takes it seriously. As for my grandparents, they look positively crushed. That's the worst part, the look on their faces. Oh, my poor mother, what's going to happen to her? I mean, I know nobody's going to beat her or anything like that, but how is she ever going to get their trust again? I know not graduating is horrible, but hurting your parents that badly and destroying their faith in you is worse, the worst thing in the world.

My grandmother doesn't say anything. She'd be the one hollering if it was just a small bit of mischief, but this is too serious, and she looks at my grandfather, who always takes charge when a big crisis comes along. Finally he says, "I'm thoroughly ashamed of you, Felicia. So is your mother. I never thought you'd do anything dishonest. That's what's so disappointing—your dishonesty."

When my grandmother hears that, tears come to her eyes. She doesn't shout or even seem to be angry, but she looks crushed, like her heart is really breaking apart. She pulls her handkerchief out of her robe pocket and pretends she's not really crying, just blowing her nose. Nobody gets fooled.

"I can't believe it, Ned." She's almost pleading with my grandfather. "There must be some other explanation. There has to be. . . . I know my child and she couldn't do anything like this. I just know it. . . ."

"Felicia?" My grandfather turns to Cici, and you can see he's hoping my grandmother is right.

"It's true. . . . I wish so hard it wasn't. But it is."

"Oh my God. . . ." Now my grandmother isn't even trying to cover her tears.

"Please, Mommy, don't," Cici says softly. "I know apologies won't help anything, but I'm sorry. I've never been so sorry for anything in my life." Then her voice gets stronger and calmer. "And I'm going to go to school and tell them the whole story. It's the only way I can make things right with myself and with you."

"No, you can't do that," says my grandfather. "You'll have no chance of graduating if you do that. Take your chances on the test. It may have been your intention to cheat, but you haven't yet. I don't think we need to make this a wide-open scandal. Maybe your mother and I can get the test postponed for you for a few extra days. We'll talk to your teacher on Monday morning."

"Please don't, Daddy," Cici says. "It's not just the test I'm thinking about. It's even more important than that— it's—I don't know, I guess it's my honor, or whatever you've got that makes people trust you. I have to prove that I still have it. Even in the beginning I knew this was more serious than cutting a class or some of the other crazy things all the kids do. This wasn't kid stuff, and now that it's all blown apart, I can't duck it like a kid." And then she turns to me and says, "I mean you have to start taking responsibility sometime."

All this time she's talking I'm thinking that she certainly doesn't sound like a kid. She sounds like a mature adult and really intelligent, and I'm very proud that she's my mother, even if she is only fourteen.

My grandfather studies her a minute. "This is a pretty grave affair," he says. "Are you sure you understand the consequences?"

"No, I'm not sure," says Cici. "But I guess it's time for me to start learning."

My grandfather and grandmother exchange a glance. There's just the tiniest bit of a smile on my grandmother's face, and I see my grandfather nod his head. "Okay, Felicia," he says, and his voice is softer now. "Everybody makes mistakes. Even grownups. Admitting them and correcting them is what's important and you're doing a very brave thing."

"That's the way I feel too, Felicia," says my grand-mother as she stands up and holds out her arms. My mother rushes into them and turns to be embraced by my grandfather.

"Just remember we're in your corner and we'll help you any way we can," he says. "And I think right at this moment both your mother and I are pretty proud of your decision."

Even Uncle Steve, who hasn't said a word, looks kind of impressed. And so am I. I don't know why there's a little lump in my throat, but there is. I know it's very bad, what she did, but still, to confess the whole story to the teacher because of her honor—it takes more guts than I would have, that's for sure.

"I'll go with you if you want, Cici." That's me speaking. Right now I'd do anything in the world to help her.

"Would you, Victoria? I'd really appreciate that." And she sort of smiles and I feel sensational.

"Do you realize what time it is?" There goes my grandmother sounding like a regular mother again. "It's almost two a.m. and these children are still up. All three of you, into bed this instant."

"Boy, she really screwed up my whole night and I got an important ball game tomorrow morning. How am I going to pitch without any sleep?" Uncle Steve is back in action again.

"Same as usual—lousy," says Cici, and my grand-mother says the usual things, and we seem to be back to normal. We all go up to bed, and I can see that it's not really back to normal at all. Cici's got this horrendous thing hanging over her head, and on top of that she's headed for 8 B or whatever they call it all over again. What a bummer!

As soon as we get into her room she starts to change into her PJ's, all the time looking away from me. I guess she's crying. I wish I could say something that would make her feel better, but I can't think of anything that isn't dumb or obviously baloney.

Without turning toward me, she hands me the folded test paper. "Here, you keep this. I don't ever want to see it again." Then, still hiding her face, she snaps out the light.

"Good night, Victoria. I'm sorry your visit turned out so badly." Even in the dark I can tell she's still crying.

"I really liked being here, Cici. I just wish there was something I could do to help you."

"Thanks. You were really keen the way you tried to take the blame. I won't forget that ever . . . ever. Victoria?"

"Yes?"

"I know this is nutty, 'cause I just met you, but right now you're the best friend I have in the whole world. I feel I could tell you anything."

"Me too," I answer, but it's not true because I know that I can't tell her the most important thing. I just can't. So I don't say anything else and neither does she, and after a while my mind begins to quiet down and just as it starts to turn gray outside, I drift off to sleep.

And I dream. Long, involved, endless chasing nightmares. Running-away stories where I hang onto cliff edges, window-sills hundreds of feet above the street, and airplane wings until finally, agonies later, the light of the sun streaming into the room pulls me out and into the warm quiet midday. A second before I open my eyes a thought shoots through my head. Where will I be? And I pray it'll be in my own bed at home, but even before I look I know I'm not. The feel of the sun on my cheek and the brightness on my eyelids—that doesn't happen in my room no matter what time it is. My room is in a court and sunlight like this never comes in. So there's no point in the guessing game, I open my eyes. Sure enough, I'm just where I was when I fell asleep, across the room from Cici, in my mother's bedroom in 1944. I know I'll never get home anymore.

## *Sixteen*

Just from the feel of it, I can tell it's afternoon. There's a little white radio clock on the night table between our beds, but it's facing my mother's side. I turn it very carefully, avoiding the globs of gum stuck to the top. Obviously this is where my mother sticks her gum before she goes to sleep. That's not bad except when you play the radio the top gets hot and then it melts down the sides and . . . ugh. My mother would flip if I did that now. I wish people didn't have to change so much.

I'm right, it's almost three o'clock. I guess we managed to use up most of the day already. Just as well, it's sure to be a gross one anyway. I slide out of bed as silently as I can, trying not to wake Cici. But she opens her eyes.

"It's okay. I was awake anyway. I just didn't feel like making it official by getting out of bed. But—well . . . you can't go crazy." And with one swoop she swings her legs up and out and lands standing next to her bed. Then she plops down again on the edge and just sits there, staring at nothing. I try to look very involved in getting dressed. Then, just like that, she snaps out of her trance and says, "I'm calling her. Right now."

"Who?"

"Horseface Davis. And I'm going to do it this minute before I change my mind." And she bolts out of the room and heads down the hall, I guess to phone. While she's gone I get dressed. Eventually I'm going to have to do something about these clothes. I mean, I can't wear the same thing every day forever. But where am I going to get the money to buy new ones?

"I did it. I called her." Cici has come back into the room, looking pretty deflated.

"What'd she say?"

"Nothing much, just that she can't see me till tonight. I'm supposed to be over there at eight-thirty. That's a long wait. . . ."

"Felicia!" my grandmother calls from downstairs. "Felicia, Victoria, breakfast!"

"We're coming right down," my mother leans out the door and shouts. Then she turns to me and shrugs. "Might as well." And we go downstairs to the kitchen, where my grandmother is making her super blueberry pancakes. Fabulous! I love them!

"I hope you like blueberry pancakes," Cici says, helping me to a couple. "These are really keen." That word "keen" always makes me want to giggle.

"Are you kidding? I love them. These are the best I've ever had."

They both look at me kind of funny because I haven't even tasted them yet. Little mistake, but easy to wiggle out of. "They have to be because I've never had homemade pancakes before. All we have at home are the frozen ones."

"Frozen pancakes? I never heard of such a thing." Now my grandmother is really interested. "Where do you buy them?"

Here goes nothing. "Actually my father picks them up in a commune in New Jersey." It's my policy to tell stories so odd that people can't find anything to hang a question on. All they can say is a polite "Oh, of course," and let it drop. That's just what my grandmother says now. I see from her face that I have to be more careful. They probably think I'm a little strange already—I mean, what with my jeans and clogs. Especially the clogs. I can see my grandmother staring at them, but I'm prepared. If she says anything I'll tell her they're orthopedic. In fact, why wait?

"They're orthopedic."

"I beg your pardon?"

"My shoes. They're orthopedic."

"Oh, of course." What'd I tell you.

"Foreign orthopedic." I know that's a little heavy, but I might as well pick up a little sympathy while I'm at it. From the way she shakes her head, I can see that I'm getting some. I finish the pancakes and tell her that they're sensational, and she gives me two more, and I think she's beginning to like me a little more. Still, how much can you like one of your daughter's friends when you only met her a day ago? It's very hard getting used to not being loved by your own family. Sometimes in the past, I mean the future, I used to think that nobody loved me. Well, now that it's really happened it's completely different. I'd never make that mistake again.

I'm so busy devouring my pancakes I don't even notice that my mother hasn't even touched hers. In fact, she's looking absolutely miserable. When she catches me looking at her, she gives me a tiny smile and then she excuses herself and leaves the kitchen. My grandmother doesn't say anything, just takes her plate off the table and makes herself busy putting things away. I finish up the last of my pancakes pretty fast and take my plate to the sink.

"That's all right, dear," says my grandmother. "I'll do

that. Why don't you go upstairs and keep Felicia company? I think she needs someone to talk to.''

"Sure thing, Mrs. Lyons.'' Wow, that's funny, I mean, calling my grandmother "Mrs. Lyons.'' "And thanks for the pancakes—they were the best I ever had.'' She smiles and I know I'm making headway.

I go upstairs and my mother is sitting on her bed sewing her grungy old graduation dress.

"Hi.'' I try to sound real casual.

"Sorry I deserted you, but I guess I'm just not so hungry.''

"Hey, don't worry about me. Really, I understand.''

"I knew you would.'' And she gives me a nice kind of confidential look. Then, motioning to the dress, she says that she's just killing time so she thought she might as well try to get the placket in, and just as soon as the words come out of her mouth she remembers that she probably won't even need the dress and, like it was on fire, she shoves it off her lap.

"Well, that's one crummy thing I won't have to do.''

"You really think she won't let you graduate?''

"Absolutely. When I tell her what I tried to do she'll probably even expel me.''

"You think so?''

She just gulps and shrugs her shoulders.

"What about Ted? She can't expel her own kid.''

"She won't have to 'cause I'm not going to tell who the other person is.''

"But he's such a . . . a bastard.''

"Still, I'm not going to rat on him.''

"But he doesn't deserve to get away with it like that.''

"Maybe not, but I'm not doing it for him, I'm doing it for me.''

"How come?''

"It's just . . . promise you won't laugh?"

I promise absolutely, because I could never laugh at my mother now when she's in such terrible trouble.

"Well, you may think this is real jerky after all the crazy things I've done, but squealing is against my ethics. For that matter, so's cheating on a science test." And she waits for me to laugh or something, but I don't because I can really understand how she feels. It's sort of like what happened with me and Liz at the party in Philly. I could have stuck Liz with that joint easy, but I didn't because it would have been like squealing, and come to think of it, that's against my ethics too. Maybe I'm a lot more like my mother than I thought. Right now I kind of hope so.

Anyway, Cici goes on. "Going against your ethics makes it sound like it's religious or something, but for me it means just not doing things that make you feel ashamed inside." For a split second there, I thought she was putting me on, but I can see she's not. Talking very seriously like this makes me a little uncomfortable so I don't make any comment. I just listen. "When you're little, there's always someone to take care of things like that, someone to tell you, no, don't do that. But when you get older, like us, you have to start taking the responsibility yourself. I was still acting like a kid. I guess I just didn't realize that it was time to stop being a kid and start growing up."

It freaks me out hearing her say those things because suddenly she's hitting pretty close to home. You could say that that's my problem too—I mean all that trouble I'm always getting into in school. So I tell her that I think she's really got it together and that in a funny way she's helped me too. That seems to make her feel a little better for a while anyway. I feel very close to her now and I can tell she feels the same about me. Maybe my grandmother's

right about responsibility changing you. Cici sounds different already.

For the next few hours we just sit around the room
rapping about all kinds of different things. Mostly we're
both trying to not think about what's going to happen. I
don't know about my mother, but it doesn't work for me.
All I can think of is that soon it's going to be eight-thirty
and we're going to have to go over to that teacher's house,
and from the sound of her, she's horrendous. My teacher,
Mrs. Serrada, is a horror, but apparently she's Mary Poppins
compared to this gnome. My mother says that Horseface is
even meaner in her sewing class than she is in science, if
that's possible. Nothing she loves better than to get some
poor schnook up there in front of the whole class and make
her cry while she rips out seams that took forever to put in.
According to Cici (who I suspect knows from firsthand
experience), one crummy little mistake and Horseface practically tears the whole dress apart. Oh, boy, I dread this
confrontation. Still, I guess that's nothing compared to the
consequences. My mother must be worrying about the
same thing because right at that moment she turns to me
and says, "I'll never live this down. I'll always be that
freak girl who didn't graduate. All my friends are going to
be in high school and I'll have nobody to talk to in my
class. I'll be just like Harold."

"Hey," I say, "that's not true. People forget quickly,
you'll see." But she doesn't buy it for a minute and she's
right. They're going to point her out like she was some
kind of weirdo.

"And then I'll never be able to go to college. But
there's no college in the whole world that'll take me with
this on my record. My whole life is probably ruined . . . I
wish . . . I wish so hard it never happened. How can I stay
here and face next year? I just can't. I can't face it." And

she squeezes her eyes tight shut for a second and then she says suddenly, "I'll leave first."

"You mean run away?"

"Right."

"But you can't just take off like that. I mean there's got to be another way."

"There isn't. Besides I've made up my mind I have to go."

"Right now?"

"Yes."

Oh, no. I can't let her do such a horrendous thing. "Cici, I think you're making a grotesque mistake."

"Look, Victoria, I only told you because you're my dearest friend and the only person in the whole world I would trust with this kind of secret, but there's no way you can talk me out of it so don't even try."

"But it's dangerous."

"It doesn't matter. I told you I made up my mind so let's not talk about it anymore. Okay?"

"Sure," I say. "I didn't mean to bug you." But all along I'm thinking that I'm not going to let her run away. No matter what.

"Forget it. It's okay."

No way! Now I'm really freaking out because I've made up my mind too. I've got to come up with some way to stop her. I mean she's my mother and she's my best friend and I'm not going to stand around doing nothing while she screws up her whole life. Damn it!

I count to forty-six slowly and then . . . "Cici?"

"Yeah?"

"What about all those things you said—you know, the stuff about not being a kid again?"

She looks surprised and then annoyed. Considering she's

my only friend in the entire world, I'm probably taking a big chance going at her like this.

Without even answering me, she grabs down an old suitcase from a shelf in her closet and starts throwing clothes in it.

"All those things you said to your parents? Just a load of BS, huh?"

"You know it wasn't, Victoria, but I . . . I just can't go through with it."

And the way she looks at me I feel sick to keep pushing her like this, but I have to stop her . . . any way I can.

"So instead you take the kid's way out. Boy, Cici, you're really too much. Your parents are going to be off the wall when they find out. Don't you care?"

"Hey, cut it out!"

"Plus now *they're* going to be stuck with the responsibility of straightening out *your* problems for the ninety millionth time."

Now she's furious. "What's it to you, anyway!"

"A lot. You fooled me like everyone else, only worse because it was like you were talking about me and doing what I should be doing—you know, taking responsibility for myself—and it made sense and I really got sold. Big yak, huh?"

From the way she stares at me, I think maybe I'm beginning to reach her a little.

"You're wrong, it wasn't baloney. I meant it," she says, "when I said it."

"Then, damn it, stick to it."

She doesn't answer, but she's not packing either.

"C'mon . . . I'll help you. I swear." I'm practically begging her. "I'll stick with you every single minute."

She just stands there staring at the half-packed suitcase, not moving, as though she's trying to decide, and then just like that she flips the top closed and shoves it out of the way. Now she looks up at me. There are tears in her eyes, but she's not crying. "I knew it all along," she says. "Growing up stinks."

And then she smiles at me.

I hope I did right. But I don't have much time to worry because suddenly, from out of nowhere, the scream of a police siren freezes me. Instantly my mother jumps up. Her face snaps into life as she shouts, "It's an air-raid alarm!"

"What? An air raid?"

"Wait here!" she says. "I gotta turn off the lights downstairs. Be right back." And she flies out of the room, knocking the stupid test paper off the dresser as she passes.

"Hey, wait for me!" I shout, but she's gone. I pick up the test paper and just sit on the bed staring at it and listening to that crazy siren wailing like it was right outside the window.

Funny, all this fuss about the test and neither of us really even looked at it before. So I look and—you're not going to believe this, but that creep stiffed her. The paper says 1943, but this is 1944, so that's last year's test he was trying to sell her. No wonder he was so hot to call it off. I told you there was something fishy about his attitude. He was ripping her off. What a bum! I shove the paper into the secret drawer. Wait till I show Cici.

"Turn those lights off," a man's voice shouts from the street. I look out the window and everything is dark so he must mean me. I leap to the switch and turn it off. I can't believe this whole thing. I mean, I keep forgetting we're at war. I know it's only a drill, but what if it's not? A bomb could drop any minute and I'm busy worrying about some dumb test paper. I gotta get my head together. I just can't sit here in total darkness on the bed like some kind of jerk waiting to be blown out of the roof. But what should I do? Hide under the bed? Fat lot of good that'll do.

"Cici! Cici!" Waste of time trying to shout over those sirens. Well, I'm certainly not going to wait up here. Any jerk knows you're supposed to go to the basement. At least it's more like an air-raid shelter down there. Where is my mother! How could she just go off and leave me like this.

"Cici!" Oh, boy, my voice is getting screechy. I'm really losing control. "Cici!" I can't help it, I'm scared, really terrified. I've got to find my mother. "Mommy!"

It's black in the house and there's no light coming from the outside so I just feel along the wall until I get to the door of the room. The hall is like the inside of my eyelids, but at least I know where the steps are so I just creep my way along the hall. If those sirens would only stop. I run my fingers along the wall and accidentally hit a small picture, and it slides off the hinge and falls to the floor. Naturally, I manage to clump right on it, crunching the glass and snapping the wood frame all in one step. I'm not about to stop for anything now, so I kick it behind me and keep going. I must be near the end of the hall by now, so I walk more carefully, slowly feeling around, making little circles with my foot, hunting around for the beginning of the stairs. I think the railing was on the right, but I don't remember. And now I can't find it. It must be farther down the hall. I have to hurry. Even if the planes were right overhead you couldn't hear them over the sirens.

"Mommy!" Stupid to call her—she couldn't possibly hear me. Ohhh, my toe goes over nothing, no floor, hurtling me forward. I grab out for the railing, for anything, but there's nothing but flat wall. My hands slide, my body falls forward and down, and I'm going through the air, banging my shoulders against the sides of the wall, slamming my hands against the steps, sliding down on my palms over the edges of the stairs, knocking, bumping, and then crashing boom against a solid wall with my forehead. Lightning strikes and painful colors push me farther and farther down until I'm spinning, pulling, pushing, then suddenly falling free and easy. Arms far out, flying gently, floating through tingly red soup, lying back and feeling numb, but good, kind of smiley goofy good. We're hanging there, the red soup and me. Far away I can make out some blue spots slowly swimming around. Blue lima beans? Hello, purple noodles, and way far up at the tippy-top, something white. The top of the pot? The something white is getting bigger and bigger as I get closer. It's round and spreading and it's bright and glaring and yellow and I'm heading right for it, and now my head bursts through it and out into the open. . . .

## Seventeen

"What happened? The bomb! Did they drop the bombs?"

"It's all right, girlie" A gentle voice with a big pink sweaty face is leaning over me. "Just take it easy, nobody dropped any bombs, just a short stop."

Ooooh, suddenly my head pounds with pain and I put my hand up to rub it and there's this gigantic bump right between my eyebrows. Wow, is that sore.

"What happened?" I ask again, and the pink face pulls back and now I recognize it. It's that old train conductor, the one who was so nice to me on the trip from Philadelphia, the first one with the big crinkly smile. And that's just what his face does now as he tells me about how the train made a short stop just at the mouth of the tunnel into New York and I must have fallen forward and banged my head against the seat in front. He says that I look okay to him except for that big red mountain growing out of the center of my forehead. Lucky me, I was the only one on the whole train who got hurt.

"Be a good idea, honey, if you tell your mother to take you to the doctor when you get home," say the lady in the next seat.

I look at her to say that I will, and it's that same old lady with the crazy red lipstick that matches her scarf and shoes, the one I thought got off the train ages ago. The train! What am I doing on the train? Where's Cici? The house? The air raid . . .

"The air raid!" I shout. "What about the air raid?" I can't quite get my head together.

"Ain't no air raid, girlie, you musta been dreaming," the conductor says, and looks at the old lady, who shakes her head in agreement.

"Take it easy, honey, everything's all right, you just got yourself a little confused from being bumped on the head. Now, you just sit back and try and relax some." And she pats me gently on the arm and there's a little jerk forward and the train begins to move again.

"She'll be okay now," the old lady says to the conductor, and he winks at me and starts to move on up the aisle.

I sit back quietly in my seat like the lady says, and try to relax. But I can't because my mind's crazy like a bowl of spaghetti, all messy tangles and slippery loose ends. So I end up not thinking, just blinking my eyes like I'm some kind of slide projector and waiting for the picture to change. But it doesn't. I keep getting the same shot of me on the train heading for New York, just like way back in the beginning, which must mean that it's like the conductor says, I was unconscious. Of course, that makes the explanation very simple. While I was knocked out I dreamed the whole thing—Cici, my grandparents, the test, the weekend, and because I'm so brilliant, 1944 and World War II. Uh-uh . . . no way! Listen, I'm not saying I'm a dummy, but I couldn't do it. I mean, I could never put together anything as real as that. How could I? Outside of the movies, I swear I don't know a thing about the forties. So how could I do it, I mean, with the clothes and the people and the war and . . . unless it was all wrong. Suppose it didn't look at all the way I pictured it, then I guess it could have been a dream. But it seemed so real and it took so long and so many things happened and . . .

The loudspeaker announces Penn Station, New York, and people all around me start gathering up their belongings. The lady next to me smiles over the top of a lapful of shopping bags, and I remember shoving my suitcase on the shelf over the seat so I say excuse me and slide past her to get it. While I'm reaching for it, I look around at the people. Most of them are standing. And you know what? They're people, I mean grownups—all those kids and babies are gone. And their clothes—well, they're regular—you know, some jeans, some dresses, no hats—regular. I still can't believe it. It seemed so real so absolutely true. It zonks me to think it was only a dream.

Hey! What am I thinking? This is great. I'm home! All that time, back there in the forties, all I wanted was to get home and see my family, and now I'm here and I can.

Maybe. All I gotta do is take one look at the information booth. If my mother's there, then I'll know I'm really home.

I really want her to be there . . . badly.

It's always slow getting off trains and up crowded staircases, but this time it's taking forever. But so far, everything's right, I mean the station looks the way it always does.

The main floor is jammed. I put my head down and burrow into the crowd and with a lot of "excuse me's" push and shove my way through. I'm so afraid to look up because if she's not there . . .

I'm practically on top of the information booth, so I sneak my head up a little just to peek. She's there! Fantastic! And she even brought Nina. Super!

"Hey, Ma! Mommy!" And I go charging for her and practically leap into her arms. At first she's stiff, like I really stunned her, which I probably did because I can't remember the last time I gave her such a greeting. Then she starts to hug me too, and this is ridiculous, but we both stand there hugging and kissing each other like we've been away for years. Boy, am I glad to see her. Even Nina. This is a terrible embarrassment, but I have to tell you that somewhere in all this loving and stuff I get so carried away that I even kiss Nina. I may never live that down.

Now my mother pulls back a little and, wouldn't you know, the first thing she sees is the bump.

"My God! What happened?" And she starts examining and fussing and throwing a million questions at me. So I explain about the short stop and she's all concerned and she doesn't even ask me about anything else, just grabs me and we go whizzing out of the station. Once in the car, she makes me sit back and not say anything. Naturally we drive directly to the doctor, who isn't exactly out of his mind with joy to do business on a Sunday, but he says it's not a concussion and I'm probably going to live. The way my mother takes me home and puts me into bed you'd think she didn't believe him. Nobody's allowed to bug me in any way. And it's lovely just to creep into my very own bed. I didn't realize how tired I was, but practically the minute I hit the pillow, I'm asleep. And best of all, no dreams.

I open my eyes slowly . . . slowly, barely peeking out from under the squint. It feels like my own room, but so far I can't see anything much. I take it very slow because I'm not up to any more surprises. I open a tiny bit more and then I see it—beautiful gray gauzy nothing. Hooray! I'm home! I told you I've got this corner room in a court that only gets sun at two o'clock in the afternoon, and even then it's used. I mean, it's reflected off a window in the next apartment house and only about four inches of it slices into my room. Anyway, right now it looks like five o'clock on a rainy afternoon in February, so I must be home.

My ecstatic joy lasts about four seconds and then all the awfuls come flooding back—the school problem, the meeting with the principal, the pot hassle down in Philadelphia. Looking from the most optimistic angle, my situation is horrendously gross and getting worse. Maybe I should pretend I'm in a coma. That could happen easy from a bump on the head. Nah, it's hopeless, I could never pull it off. One look at Nina or someone like that and I'd surely start to laugh. Besides comas are bad news, I mean, you can't even scratch yourself. On the other hand, amnesia is perfect. You can do anything you want and nobody can blame you for anything. It's like starting all over again with no black marks against you. It'd take me ten years to accumulate all those minus points, and by then I'd be almost twenty-four and out from under. I mean, what do you say to a twenty-four-year-old who smokes pot or makes a little noise in the movies?

"Victoria!" Like they say in the confession magazines, it's the voice of truth. Actually, it's only my mother.

"Victoria!" It's coming closer. You know what? I swear it sounds a smidgen like Cici, but, of course, it was my dream so I probably gave her my mother's voice.

"Victoria!" I'm beginning to get vibes of slight concern in her voice. She turns on the light. "What's the matter?" Heavy concern, working into big worry, bordering on panic. "Victoria!" She rushes to my bed.

"Yeah." I can't do it. I'm too chicken for amnesia.

"Are you deaf?" All that deep beautiful concern is immediately replaced by plenty of angry impatience. "What are you waiting for? Don't you know we have an appoint-

ment with the principal at nine? Aren't things bad enough?
Do you want to be late on top of everything?''

She rattles off eight more questions on the same order.
All of which I answer by oozing slowly out of bed and
reaching for my clothes. I'm not too chicken to rub my
bump a little, even though, my luck, there's not a trace of
it left. If it were a pimple, it'd be there for a week. The
little rub works good enough anyway. In fact, too good—
now she's starting to help me dress. All almost-fourteen-
year-olds just love to be dressed by their mothers. I never
win.

Breakfast is strange, not terrible, just different. It's just
my mother and me. My father's already left for the office
and Nina's gone to school. My mother doesn't even make
me eat breakfast, and she doesn't say a word when I don't
take milk or anything. The four-block walk to school is
weird, too. Total silence. Nothing. Not even some helpful
hints about how I should behave with the principal or
threats about what's in store for me if he doesn't take me
back. She doesn't even hassle me about the pot business at
Liz's party. Not one blessed thing. I'm beginning to feel
very creepy. I mean, I was nervous before, but now . . . it
may be heavier than I thought. I've got this bad feeling
about my mother. A terrible feeling. Like she's given up
on me.

# *Eighteen*

By the time we get to the school, classes have started and the halls are deserted. Everybody's where they're supposed to be, except me. I'm the strange one and I don't like the feeling. I wish I hadn't done all those dumb things. I wish I had been more like everyone else. Even the pot thing, if I hadn't always gotten into all the other trouble, nobody would have thought to blame me for that. Maybe it's like Cici said; I'm getting too old for this kind of stuff. Sure I know I'll never be a goody-goody like Margie Sloan, but it may be time to cool things a bit. I mean a couple of fun nutty things once in a while is okay, but three times a week was too much. I can see that now. Naturally it's too late. To tell you the truth, if I could get out of this whole thing right now, I'd be so perfect I'd make Margie Sloan look like a junkie.

Miss Olerfield, the principal's secretary, looks out of her head with joy to see me bringing my mother. She knows it means trouble and she's hated me since the gum-on-the-seat incident from the fourth grade. I can't understand people like that who hold a grudge forever.

"Mrs. Martin," she says, "Mr. Davis is waiting for you." And then to me, "I think we can manage a little tiny greeting now, can't we, Victoria?"

"Sorry, Miss Olerfield, I was watching the roach climbing into your pocketbook."

Freak-out squeals, leaps, and lunges as she flings the entire contents of her bag all over the desk and floor. I want to stop to help her pick it up, but my mother grabs me by the arm and leads me into Mr. Davis's office before I can even offer. From the way she grips my arm, maybe she hasn't given up on me completely.

Mr. Davis gets up from behind his super-neat, absolutely empty desk (nobody's ever figured out exactly what a principal does except maybe aggravate kids and their parents) to greet us. He's a real winner, tall and skinny and twelve months pregnant. At least that's what his belly looks like. He's always dressed in dusty brown suits, even when they're blue. He's musty, dull, and tacky. I'm crazy about him.

"Mrs. Martin?" He puts out his hand to my mother. "I don't believe I've had the pleasure."

"Mr. Davis?" my mother says, then suddenly stops dead.

And so does he.

"Ted . . . Ted Davis?" My mother looks stunned.

Ted Davis! I don't believe it! Like in my dream. It can't be.

"Cici? Are you Cici Lyons?" His eyes are practically popping. "Don't tell me you're Cici Lyons. I don't believe it."

Lucky they're not looking at me because I'm totally flipped out.

I mean, it was only a dream.

It can't have happened. It was only from the bump on my head.

But Cici and Ted? How did I know? I couldn't have unless—*unless I was there.*

"My, my, what a lot of years." Mr. Davis is shaking his head in disbelief.

"Thirty years? No, more, my goodness," says my mother. "All that time. But I swear, you look almost the same. You do."

Of course, she's lying, I'd never have recognized him. Then he gives her the bull how she looks the same too, and then they go into a whole long thing about what this one is doing and how that one got divorced three times and that one ran for Congress and someone else moved to Alaska and on and on and I don't recognize any of the names yet.

"I can still see Pop Stiller's malt shop."

I know that name. I'm sure I do. I think my mother mentioned it when she told me about how Ted offered her the test the first time. I know she said she was in some malt shop and I could swear it was Pop somebody's. I think I'm going bananas because maybe I really was there.

"It's been gone for years. They tore down the whole block and built a huge apartment house."

Who cares about that? Get to the test thing.

"What about the school?"

"Gone too."

The test. What about the test!

"I have some pretty grim memories of that place," says my mother.

I know one for sure.

"Don't we all."

If they don't get to that damn test, I'm going to ask them myself. I swear I don't care, I have to know.

"You know, Ted, I've never forgiven you for that thing you pulled on me."

Suddenly I'm afraid. Up till now I was dying to know, but now I'm afraid. But it's too late to stop them now.

"I know that was awful and I felt terrible afterward, but . . ."

"I could have killed you."

"I never should have run off and left you like that . . ."

"Ooooh . . ." That was me. I didn't mean to, but it just slipped out. They both look at me.

A pinprick of silence, then Mr. Davis goes on. " . . . at the party."

Party? What's he talking about? He wasn't even at that party.

"At the party?" My mother's shaking her head and looking straight at me. "Oh, yes," she suddenly says. "The party. Deserting me at that miserable party to come home all by myself at midnight. My parents were furious."

He didn't leave her at any party. What are they talking about? Don't they remember? He ran off . . . when we all fell trying to get back into the house . . . the police, the test . . . he whole thing.

"I should have taken you home. I'm really sorry."

They're lying. They don't want me to know. They were going to say it, then they noticed me and they changed the whole story. The party business is baloney. I know it . . . I know it . . . I know it. . . .

"Victoria, please, dear, don't cry . . . it's all right."

My mother is holding me and I can't stop sobbing and shaking. Now they're both fussing over me. I wish I could control myself but I can't. . . .

"It's all right . . . everything's going to be okay." She's still hugging me, and even though it feels good, I can't seem to stop sobbing. "Victoria's not herself today. She had a slight accident on the train coming from Philadelphia yesterday. Just a bump on the head, but I think it upset her."

It's not that. It's just such a huge letdown. I absolutely

convinced myself that it was all only a dream, and then this stuff happens with my mother and Mr. Davis and I start freaking out all over again. I guess it's because I wanted so hard for it to be true—I mean, about how it was with my mother and me back then. We were so close and it felt so good and now it's all gone and she's just my mother again and we're right back where we started . . . a million miles apart.

"Poor child." Mr. Davis puts his head out the door and asks Miss Olerfield to get me a glass of water. While we're waiting for the water, Mr. Davis, never one to miss a chance to kick someone when they're down, starts right in on me. He pulls out my records and begins reading off all my crimes. What seems like four days later, he's still reading. Lucky they don't have firing squads in schools. A lot of the things I can't remember. On the other hand, a lot I can and some of them are beginning to strike me funny, which can be very dangerous. All I need now is to be struck by the laughing bit.

"As you can see this presents an impossible situation," Mr. Davis tells my mother. "We're simply not equipped to deal with these kinds of disruptions and still give the other four hundred students the education they deserve. We must eliminate the incorrigibles."

At least I didn't think they had firing squads.

"And I'm afraid your daughter qualifies as an incorrigible. We have tried to deal with her time and again, but don't seem to get through to her. She is a constant troublemaker. Not only does she create problems for herself, but she leads the other children astray. We cannot have that kind of influence in our school."

Okay, so maybe I am a troublemaker, sort of, but still I don't think I influence anybody else except maybe jerks like Tina Osborne—and practically anybody could influence her.

"One minute, Ted." Up till now my mother's just been listening. "I agree we're dealing with a difficult situation here, but you must admit most of the incidents are more childish than dangerous. When you talk about leading the other students astray, you make it sound almost evil. My daughter's actions are certainly foolish, but hardly immoral."

"A foolish child often becomes an immoral adult."

"I don't think that follows at all."

"It's been my experience—"

"It's been my experience that all children are foolish at times. Don't you agree?"

"Well . . . it's true that children can be foolish, but in this case it's constant."

It looks hopeless. I'm sort of surprised to see how my mother's really coming on strong for me, but still I think he's made up his mind to throw me out and that's that. But boy, it would be so great if she could only get me out of this mess . . . just this one last time. Actually, I probably used up my last time about five hundred times ago. Wait a minute. It just hit me that I'm acting like a kid, waiting for my mother to fix everything. This whole business is a lot like when Cici wanted to run away and I talked her into staying and taking responsibility for dealing with her own problems. That was fabulous advice considering I never even tried it myself. Maybe it's time I did.

"Excuse me . . ." I practically whisper it, but they both stop talking instantly and turn to me. "Uh . . . I know saying I'm sorry won't change things, but . . ."

"It certainly won't," says Mr. Davis. "It's much too late for apologies. You'd have done well to consider your actions before you took them and not hope to get by with apologies later."

"But . . ." He's so gross he doesn't even let me finish talking.

"People like you always think you can get by without paying the piper—well, you're going to learn, young lady, that you've got to pay and the price is high."

God. Cici was right. Growing up stinks, still I make one last try. "I know, Mr. Davis, but . . ."

"No buts about it. . . ." And he's off and running.

"Ted." My mother interrupts in her shut-your-mouth-right-this-minute voice.

It works.

"Why not let the child finish her sentence?"

"Of course, Victoria, go right ahead." He says it like it was all his idea.

"Uh . . ." That's me again, the groper. "Uh . . . I only meant to say, you're right, Mr. Davis. There's no room in this school for someone who does the dumb things I do." Suddenly I have tears in my eyes. "And I really want to stay in this school so I'm not going to do them anymore." I'm swallowing hard.

Now even my mother looks surprised. Still, neither of them make any comment so I bring in the big guns. "I've outgrown it, that's all. Making that kind of trouble is kid stuff and I'm just too big for it now." I hold my breath and wait.

My mother recovers first. "Victoria, that's the best news I've had in ages." And she looks like she really means it.

"Well, now—" Mr. Davis doesn't seem all that convinced. "Of course, that's easy to say . . ."

But my mother is. "No, it's not, Ted, it's really quite difficult. And I'm very proud of you, Victoria." That makes me feel super. And then to Mr. Davis: "I really think she's come up with the perfect answer to the problem. Don't you, Ted?'' She's really pushing for me.

''Well, I don't know . . .''

''Well, I do, especially when I think of all the mistakes we made as kids . . . you do remember your mistakes, don't you?'' Now she sounds like the Godfather.

And it works. He's remembering. ''On the other hand, it does sound like a mature decision. . . .''

''You certainly have a point there,'' says my mother, egging him on.

''Yes, sir, it seems to me we may have come up with the perfect answer to our problem.''

''I couldn't agree with you more, Ted.''

''In my judgment, and remembering that all children are prone to mistakes at some time . . .''

''You think Victoria deserves another chance.'' My mother's not taking any.

''. . . I think Victoria deserves another chance.''

Fabulous! Super! Fantastic!

''What do you think, Victoria?'' Mr. Davis asks, sticking his head toward me like a giant turtle.

Unreal. I mean, what does he think I think? I'm tempted to give it to him a little and say, ''Hey, no, don't give me another chance,'' but that would be slipping back to the baby stuff, so I catch myself and with great maturity mumble, ''Gee, thanks.''

Now my mother jumps in with another couple of tons of baloney about what a wise decision he's making and how he's probably responsible for redirecting my whole life. She stops just before she buries us all, and with a whole string of wonderful-to-see-you-agains and we-must-get-togethers, we leave, colliding with Miss Olerfield, who's finally come back with the life-saving water, which naturally goes flying all over the front of her dress.

"Oh, dear," my mother says, "we're so sorry. We didn't see you."

"It's nothing," Miss Good Sport snaps, practically biting my mother's head off.

"Don't bother getting me another glass, Miss Olerfield," I say sweetly. "I'm feeling much better now."

You can see her mentally adding this to the gum on the seat.

"And Miss Olerfield?" You can't expect me to resist every temptation. "I hope you find that roach in your bag."

My mother has me down the hall and out of the building so fast I never even got to see Miss Olerfield's reaction. Well, next time. Except now, maybe there isn't going to be any next time, what with the new me. Growing up may be harder than I thought.

Once outside the building my mother lets out a "whew!" of relief and just leans back against the school wall. She looks really beat.

"Am I glad that's over," she says. "I don't think I got two hours' sleep this whole weekend worrying about that meeting."

"But I was the one who was in trouble."

"True. But I happen to be responsible for you so it's as much my problem as it is yours."

"I didn't think of it that way."

"That's 'cause you're not a mother. Sometimes when I'm dealing with one of your endless arguments with Nina or some godawful new trouble in school or reminding you for the four billionth time to clean your bedroom, I think I'm not either. Times like that I feel more like a prison matron than a mother. And it makes me every disappointed with myself."

"I guess maybe I am a lot of trouble . . ."

"I don't know, maybe I just don't have the right approach. You won't believe this, Victoria, but when I was your age I was convinced that when I grew up I was going to be the most fantastic mother in the whole world. I would really understand my kids because I'd remember what it was like for me. But things change and I don't know—I guess you forget."

"I kind of think you did a little."

"On the other hand . . . you certainly can be a terror."

"Used to be. I've absolutely changed completely. Almost."

"Well, you were pretty terrific this morning, and even if the 'new you' doesn't make it all the way through the whole afternoon, it's still encouraging, and it certainly does wonders for my memory. Which reminds me, Ted Davis is a fink creep."

"Huh?" For a second I thought my mother called the principal a fink creep.

"Fink creep. Always was and always will be."

Wow! She did. I turn around to double-check because it sounded just like Cici. And she smiles at me and says, "I think he's one big jerko." And then in a perfect imitation of Mr. Davis's voice, "What do you think, Victoria?"

I think I may be losing my marbles, but this opportunity doesn't come every day, so I take advantage of it. "Absolutely gross!"

"Not bad. How about geek?"

"I don't know that one, but it sounds foul."

"It is. Now I was always partial to goofball for Ted."

"What about grubby freak?"

"Very nice. Although I think I'd throw in wisenheimer too."

"Okay then, how's grungy, disgusting, raunchy, horrendous, horrific, outrageous . . ."

". . . Sneaky chicken bastard!" And she says it so loud two old ladies passing by stop to give her a dirty look. Imagine if they knew she was talking about my principal. She doesn't seem to care at all. In fact, she smiles and grabs my hand tightly.

"Ouch! That hurt."

"What's wrong?"

Oh my God, the splinter from the tree! "I have a splinter in my hand," I say feebly.

"Let me see." And she examines it closely. "Where'd you get that?"

I got that, mother dear, the night we sneaked out to meet Ted to buy your science test with stolen USO money. You must remember, that was the night Ted—or should I call him Mr. Davis?—tried to get you to "put out"—of course, that was before the police caught us. I could say all that and more, but for once in my life I'm going to play it smart. I'm keeping my mouth shut. Besides, nobody wants to hear about anyone else's dreams. As for the splinter, I could have had it for days and not noticed and then it just worked its way into my dream. That happens, you know, if you hurt your foot for real, you can go limping around in your sleep. And Ted's name? Why shouldn't I know it? Everybody knows their principal's name. Even all those other things I seemed to know about my mother—well, she could have told me them over the years, like I always knew my dresser was a hand-me-down and that she lived in a house, not an apartment. Besides, I would be a real jerk to ruin what I have going now. This started out to be the worst day in my life and now it's looking great. Not only did good old Mr. Davis, the freak creep, redirect my entire life by saving me from boarding school, but my mother and I have never had it so good.

She nearly flipped me out the way she stood up for me

with Mr. Davis. And now, walking home, we have it together for the first time—we're really hitting something special. Neither of us said anything much, just that fooling around calling the principal names, but I know we both felt it. Comfortable and easy and liking each other, just the way it used to be with Cici and me. . . .

"Just soak it."

"Huh?"

"The splinter."

"Oh, yeah."

"Or you can wait for Daddy. He's brilliant with splinters. All he needs is a needle and one two three, it's out."

"I'll soak it."

"I thought you would." And she smiles a nice smile at me. When we reach home, she says, "You must be starving. What can I make for you?"

"Blueberry pancakes." I swear that just slipped out.

"You're in luck. I happen to have a box of fresh blueberries."

"I was only kidding. You don't have to bother."

"My pleasure, kiddo."

"Far out! I'll be back in a minute—just let me throw on my jeans. " And I shoot into my bedroom. I'm practically on the ceiling, I feel so high. Everything in my room looks fabulous. I love everything and everybody, my dresser, my mirror, my mother, everything. I slip my skirt off and pick up my jeans (did you think they were hanging up?) and jump into them. Even the girl in the mirror isn't so bad. I must have hit the one day in the whole year when there isn't even a sign of a pimple. At least not from ten feet across the room, and I'm not pushing my luck by going any closer. A zip and a snap and I'm ready. Looking very spiffy, Victoria, except for that gorgeous cigarette burn right in the middle of your T-shirt. Just big enough to ruin everything. Well, nothing to do but change it. Naturally, all my other shirts are in the laundry for a change. Fortunately I still have my friend Steffie's shirt I borrowed three and a half months ago when she borrowed my suede jacket, which she practically lives in, so I don't feel so bad about never returning her shirt. It's stuffed way back in the corner of my secret drawer and when I pull it out a paper comes up from under the drawer lining. So I take it out.

And I unfold it.

And I'm blitzed! I mean, absolutely wiped out! Here it is, black-and-white proof, except my hands are shaking so hard it's more like a gray blur.

Look at me going on like some kind of nut. You don't even know what I'm talking about, unless you guessed already. I wish you did, then I wouldn't have to say it, because . . . forget it, I'm saying it anyway.

Right smack in front of me is a 1943 science test!

"Victoria! It's ready. C'mon while they're hot."

For the last three days all I keep doing is trying to pull myself together. Now here I am, trying again. This time there's nothing to do but go inside and eat the blueberry pancakes that I've just lost my appetite for. Fortunately you can't tell by looking that my mind has just been practically totaled. I'm pretty good at hiding things when I want to play it cool.

"My God, Victoria, what happened?"

Well, not so much from my mother. "Nothing. I'm just happy that I don't have to go to boarding school."

"You look more shocked than happy."

"I guess I am. I really thought I was a goner."

"I'm glad it worked out. I like having you home."

My appetite may be picking up a bit. Imagine fresh blueberry pancakes twice in two days.

"They're every bit as good as Grandma's."

"I was worried that I forgot how. I haven't made them in such a long time." Then she looks at me. "I have to make them more often."

I think I may be in love.

"Mommy?"

"Umm."

"What really happened about that party?" I could never leave well enough alone.

"Nothing."

"But Mr. Davis said . . . ."

"I thought we agreed what Ted Davis was."

"Right, but . . ."

"So do I look like the kind of person that would date a gross wisenheimer jerko?"

Boy, it really is just like being with Cici. Remember, back there when I said how fabulous it would be to have someone like her for a mother?

"Absolutely not," I say.

"Actually the whole story is completely different, but I think he was too embarrassed to say it and I don't blame him. It's not exactly a great reference for a principal. I'll tell you if you're ready to accept the fact that your own mother wasn't exactly a perfect child one hundred percent of the time."

"I think I can handle it."

"Hang on to your hat. I once tried to cheat on a science test."

"No kidding?"

I guess I played it too surprised because now she wiggles out a little. "Of course, I was much younger than you are."

"How much?" I nail her because I know I'm never going to get this chance again.

"Let's see—it was 1944, I think—" She kind of giggles.

"A month and a half. Actually I've managed to block most of what happened because it really was a very unhappy experience. But I can't block out the fact that I did try to buy a science test from guess who?"

"Mr. Davis?"

"The freak creep himself. Only I got caught and he didn't and it was awful because I thought they wouldn't let me graduate."

"What happened?"

"I went to see the teacher and told her the whole story, all except the part about her own son, Ted, being the person who stole the test to sell to me. She kept asking me who it was, but I wouldn't tell. I had this thing about squealing. Anyway it paid off because somehow she knew all along that it was Ted and she was very impressed with my sense of loyalty plus the fact that I had come forward and confessed voluntarily. Maybe it helped that Ted lied and tried to get away with it. Whatever the reason, she let me graduate, but she really fixed old Ted's wagon. He got shipped off to one of those oppressive military academies. I haven't thought of that incident in years, but today seeing Ted Davis brought it all back. I remembered for the first time in too long what it felt like to be thirteen and in trouble. That's why I wanted to make sure he gave you another chance."

"I appreciate it."

"I know just how you feel. This time I really do." And she pops a kiss on the top of my head.

"I found this." And I give her the paper because now I have to see it through to the end.

She unfolds it and looks at it. Then she stares, stunned in absolute shock. And her face starts to get blotchy red and fills with fury.

Why did I show her that stupid test?

She looks up at me hard like she's seeing right into my brain. Now I've ruined everything.

"Where did you find this?"

How can I tell her? It's too bizarre and maybe she'll hate me for it, for being there and seeing all those things she wants to forget. Or she might think I was lying. . . .

"I found it in the secret drawer in my dresser. Way far in the back."

"Of course, that was once my dresser. Bum!"

"I'm sorry." Here come the tears.

"Oh, honey, not you," and she gives me a big squeeze and laughs, not really so angry anymore. "It's that Ted Davis. That ratfink cheated me. This paper says 1943! He tried to sell me a year-old test paper. Can you imagine, cheating a cheater! How do you like that?"

Of course, I forgot, she didn't know. She never saw the paper because I put it in the secret drawer during the air-raid alarm.

"I think maybe I'll send him the test and ask for my money back."

"He'd really freak out."

"On second thought, I think I'll save it as a reminder. Sometimes it's useful to remember what it's like to be a kid."

I'm feeling super-good now because I know there really has been a change. Things are going to be better from now on. Mostly I guess because of Cici. Probably every mother has a Cici someplace deep inside her if you can only find it. Unless, gross thought, when you do it turns out to be a Margie goody-goody Sloan instead. What a bummer that would be. Well, for sure no Margie Sloan ever got within a hundred miles of my mother.

I'm just standing there lapping it all up with this big goofy smile on my face.

"What's so funny?" my mother asks.

"Nothing. I just feel good."

"Me too." And her smile is almost as goofy as mine. "How about running across to Schrafft's and picking up some hot fudge and we'll make sundaes?"

"Great," I tell her, and she gives me two dollars and I head for the door.

# *Nineteen*

"Maaa . . ."

That wasn't me. The troll is home.

"Where are you going?" She always has to know everything.

"Out."

"Maa, where's she going?"

Of course my mother has to tell her, and naturally she just can't wait to have some, and there goes what was going to be a perfect day. Even hot fudge tastes like boiled liver if you have to sit at the same table with the grunge. P.S., she's still wearing my socks.

"You better walk Norman before you go," she announces.

"It's not my turn."

"It is too. I walked him for the whole weekend while you were away."

"So what. You were supposed to. I walked him before I left on Friday, and Sunday was my turn but you owed me a time so you have to walk him today."

"I don't owe you any turn."

"You do too. Remember Thursday I walked him for you when you said you sprained your finger and you told Mommy you couldn't hold the leash?"

"I couldn't, and besides it was your turn anyway."

"Wrong again, creep, Wednesday was my turn."

"But Mommy took him to the vet on Wednesday."

"So . . . lucky for me."

"That's no fair."

"Tough."

"Asshole." I don't know where eleven-year-olds pick up that kind of language.

Norman is basically a wonderful dog and I love him to pieces except that mostly he's incredibly lazy and stupid and like everyone else in this house (except me) he over-reacts, so when he hears the word "out" he goes berserk and starts barking and throwing himself at the door. Naturally, my mother hears the pounding and comes in from the kitchen to see what Norman is making such a fuss about.

"It's because Victoria won't take him out," Big Mouth says.

"It's not my turn, Mommy."

"Somebody, *anybody*, walk him *please*."

"Not me," Nina says.

"Me neither," I say, and I explain very logically why it's Nina's turn. I'm not coming on like a baby, it's person-to-person stuff, and my mother is listening, and I can feel it's our new relationship, and she keeps shaking her head, and I can see Nina's dying. Things are really going to be different from now on. I can tell. If only Norman would stop yowling.

"Victoria dear . . ."

Good start, Ma.

"I'm sure you understand that this isn't the time for a long discussion . . ."

That's reasonable.

". . . the dog must go out right now."

On cue Norman lunges for his leash.

". . . And since you were away all weekend, you take him out."

"But it's Nina's . ..."

"Now."

I can't believe she could do this horrendous thing to me after all we've been through.

"It's no fair." So what if it sounds baby.

"I said *now*."

It's useless. Hopeless. Nothing's changed. I have no choice. I hate to do it, but I have to. . . . "Make her take off my socks."

With terrifying calm my mother silently holds the door open for me. Then she turns to Nina and quietly says, "Empty the dishwasher."

"It's not my turn." Nina practically whispers.

"And set the table. And Nina?"

"Yeah?"

"TAKE OFF THOSE SOCKS RIGHT THIS MINUTE!" Then she turns to me with a smile, a different look, and says, "I haven't forgotten our hot fudge . . . or anything else."

"I'm on my way," I say happily, and Norman and I start out the door.

"Victoria?"

Uh-oh . . .

"Put on your jacket, it's only May."

"Ah, Ma!"

"On second thought, you decide."

"Sure thing, Ma," I say good and loud. And then, real soft . . . "Thanks, Cici."

# Judy Blume

Judy Blume <u>knows</u> about growing up. She has a knack for going right to the heart of even the most secret problems and feelings. You'll always find a friend in her books—like these from Laurel-Leaf!

| | | |
|---|---|---|
| ___ARE YOU THERE, GOD? IT'S ME, MARGARET...... | 90419-6-62 | $2.50 |
| ___BLUBBER.......................... | 90707-1-14 | 2.50 |
| ___DEENIE.............................. | 93259-9-69 | 2.50 |
| ___IT'S NOT THE END OF THE WORLD.............. | 94140-7-29 | 2.50 |
| ___STARRING SALLY J. FREEDMAN AS HERSELF...................... | 98239-1-55 | 2.75 |
| ___THEN AGAIN, MAYBE I WON'T................................ | 98659-1-15 | 2.50 |
| ___TIGER EYES.......................... | 98469-6-31 | 2.95 |

## ═══LAUREL-LEAF BOOKS═══

At your local bookstore or use this handy coupon for ordering:

**DELL READERS SERVICE—Dept B576B**
**P.O. BOX 1000, PINE BROOK, N.J. 07058**

Please send me the above title(s). I am enclosing $_____ (please add 75¢ per copy to cover postage and handling). Send check or money order—no cash or CODs. Please allow 3-4 weeks for shipment. CANADIAN ORDERS: please submit in U.S. dollars.

Ms./Mrs./Mr._____

Address_____

City/State_____ Zip_____